Sister Raven

Karen Rae Levine

*An original fantasy based on the culture
and customs of fifteenth-century
Native New England*

Bound by magic to Old Mother, Beetle Girl lives a lonely life on the fringes of her Native American society. When forced into the role of Keeper of the Ravens, she must break the bonds of her cruel mother, confront a powerful shape-shifter who threatens to destroy the village, and solve the mystery of her past.

visit

www.KarenRaeLevine.com

Sister Raven

Karen Rae Levine

Best wishes
Karen Rae Levine

Second Edition © 2012 Karen Rae Levine
ISBN 978-14-7925-455-2

First Edition © 2010 Karen Rae Levine
ISBN 978-05-5741-144-3

1. Indians of North America—Fiction
2. Indians of North America—New England—Fiction
3. Ravens—Fiction
4. Religion and Spirituality—Fiction

For my husband,
Matthew

and my children,
Amanda, David, and Andrew

I know my way in the darkness and duck into the familiar thicket. I have hollowed the earth just beneath this hiding place and worn a faint path to it from the hillside trail, so that my braid does not get caught on the twigs and thorns as often as it had before. I lie on my belly, with my head raised, and move nothing but my eyes.

To the right, the dark curve of Raven Keeper's lodge breaks the shadows of the trees. To the left, through the tangle of black branches, Spirit Mountain looms—a great, dark mass, outlined by the star-filled sky.

The bark-covered doorway of the lodge swings open and Raven Keeper's braid sways as she stoops through the opening. A shadow figure in the darkness, she stands as straight as a mighty pine and faces the mountain. The thrill that sweeps my body has not weakened since the first time my mother sent me here to spy.

Yellow shafts of morning break from the crook where the mountain meets the valley. Spirit Mountain grows rounder with the light. I hold my breath, waiting for Raven Keeper to begin. She faces away from me and cups her hands around her mouth. Her mournful song begins deep in her throat and rumbles past her tongue—Raven Keeper calls the ravens.

"Craw-cree-craw-cree-craw-craw!"

I tell myself to study the sound, to know it so well that I can train my throat to own it. But every time I hear it, I think I can never own that sound—that sound will always own me. It melts into my body. It grabs hold of my heart and chokes my breath. It fills my head and pushes hot tears from my eyes.

"Craw-cree-craw-cree-craw-craw!"

The last notes of Raven Keeper's song float away and I am released. I would like to drop my head and fall into sobs. It takes all my strength to be still. I blink the salt water from my eyes. If tears blind me, I will not see them.

The ravens.

Six dots speckle the snowy mountaintop, so far away I wonder if I only imagine them. Six black spots fall around each other like leaves in the wind—larger and larger, closer and closer. The ravens talk to each other, chattering all at once. "Craw!" "Cree!" "Craw!" They dance and swoop to the hill, to the clearing where Raven Keeper waits. She raises her arms and they circle around her. They call to her, greet her. Their wings brush her hands.

Then six ravens scatter to the trees.

Raven Keeper turns and stoops to enter her lodge. For a moment I see her face in the new light of day. It is a face at once full of peace and full of sadness. It is a face that has seen many moons, but is not so very old. No woman, I think, is more beautiful than Raven Keeper. I want to run to her now, to fall at her feet. *Please, please, let me live with you. I am not very good but I will help you as best I can and not be any trouble.*

But fear of my mother keeps me hidden.

A beetle scurries across my fingers. In my mind, I give the creature a greeting of respect, for I have its name. In the village, they call me Beetle Girl because I scamper around the hut I share with my mother—or so they say. I do not mind the insect, or the name, although I am no longer a girl. It will soon be the second Planting Moon I spend in the cycle of womanhood.

The beetle burrows into a pile of brown leaves as I back out of the bracken, careful not to snap a twig or catch the fringe of my skirt. Some days I stay longer to watch Raven Keeper grind acorns or roast meat. Some days I come later to watch her shape dampened cornmeal in her palms and bury the patties in hot ashes. Some days I return at dusk to watch the ravens fly back to the mountain, clutching small sacks or baskets filled with her fine food. But not today.

I have no fear of seeing another person as I make my way to the larger path that leads down the hill. It is a sacred path, used only once in each cycle of Grandmother Moon, on the day after she shows her full face. On that day, Gray Wolf leads six villagers laden with baskets. The burden-baskets contain food and supplies for Raven Keeper and the offerings change with the seasons—dried meat in the winter, fish and maple sugar in the spring, wild rice in the summer, corn and squash at the fall harvest.

Where my path touches the edge of the hill, I pause to rub my ankle. I have again outgrown the leather anklet that I have worn since before I can remember and its white beads cut my skin. I must ask my mother to make it looser.

Below me, to the west, the lodges of the village cast long, oval shadows. The domed shelters, with small garden patches scratched around them, puff feathers of gray smoke. The village yawns and wakes. A mother appears from within and greets Grandfather Sun with a face uplifted. A naked toddler wobbles past the hide of a deer stretched for tanning. A grandfather squats at a basin and splashes water on his face. A yellow dog thrusts its rump in the air and stretches its body.

To the north, planting fields carpet the land. They are brown and bare, just softening from the winter. Beyond them, wisps of smoke rise from a blackened meadow, recently cleared. Behind me, to the east, hills and forests stretch to Spirit Mountain. Southward, the river curves around the hill, almost out of my view.

West, north, east, and south. In these four directions I sense the crude outline of my life. But the circle is flat—without meaning. From this height, the four directions taunt me. They point away and hint at a far-reaching circle of possibilities— depths I have yet to imagine.

I usually find my way home through the woods, but this morning, as it is on some mornings, the sting of my solitude is sharp. I make a winding journey through the village instead, past bare-footed sisters and sleepy-eyed sons, and pretend that this smell, or that sound, belongs to me—to my life, as I dream it could be.

Little Foot, a girl of my age, pushes aside the buckskin doorway of her lodge and sticks her pinched face outside. With the bark dome behind her, I think she looks like a great turtle, and I smile.

"Where have you been so early?" she says.

I cannot answer her. I must not tell anyone where I go before dawn. From the time I was a little girl, it has been my mother's wish that I become the keeper of the ravens—that I replace Raven Keeper on that hill. I have never understood how this could be so, but I have always understood that no one must ever know.

How I would love to look upon the face of a friend! But it is the nature of friends to share intimacies, and it is difficult to exchange handfuls of pebbles while bearing the weight of a heavy stone.

I turn my eyes away and walk on without a word.

"No man will want such a proud girl for a wife!" Little Foot releases the buckskin and withdraws into her turtle shell.

Tomorrow I will find my way home through the woods.

The lodge I share with Old Mother, as my mother is called, is set away from the others, the last before the planting fields. Her herb garden merges with the shrubs and young pines that border the woods. Like the beetle, I burrow into the lodge, but once inside, a sour odor makes me pause. A tall clay pot leans against the fire stones and a root of some sort boils within it.

I hold the buckskin flap and Old Mother winces at the light I let into our tiny lodge.

"*Aye-kye!*" she groans. "Close the door, clumsy one." She leans over a flat stone and cuts thin slices of the stinking root with her bone knife.

We are not alone. A woman sits in the shadows with her hands tight on the shoulders of a small, wide-eyed boy. They have come, as others do, in need of healing. But they are frightened and would not have come unless their own remedies had failed. People in the village are wary of my mother, and some call her Witch.

Old Mother grinds the root. Her face has the texture of a walnut and the coarse hair that frames it is black and white together. Around her neck she wears a string of pointed roots used for healing. Hanging this way, they have the appearance of a necklace of claws.

With gnarled fingers, Old Mother applies patches of the paste to sores on the boy's chest and back. The woman gasps when my mother brings the knife to the boy's skin. But Old Mother chuckles and presses the flat of the knife to one poulticed sore, and then to the next. The woman leaves a wooden bowl as payment for the treatment and hurries from the hut with her son.

My mother waves the bowl. Carved from the hard burl of a tree, its rich, swirling grain shines in the firelight. Many hours, I can see, went into its making.

"This is all the thanks I get," says Old Mother, "when she knows no other could help her little runt."

Because she spends so many hours inside, Old Mother's

back has the curve of the lodge walls. Outside, she stoops to tend her herb garden, but then cannot stand completely upright. I spend as little time inside as possible and practice standing as straight as the pines, as tall as Raven Keeper.

"Did you listen to her?" asks my mother.

"Yes, Mother."

She grins. Her teeth are strong and they shine in the firelight. "Did you practice the call?"

"I will, later." I sit on a mat by the fire and extend my leg. "Please, will you loosen it?"

Old Mother takes my ankle in her cold hands. With closed eyes, she presses her bone knife flat against the knot. Many times have I pulled at the knot without success. Many times have I pushed a flint knife across the leather, with no result. Even the quill of a porcupine could not penetrate it. Old Mother opens her eyes and pulls loose the knot. There is magic in the bone knife and beaded band that I do not understand.

"Girls in the village talk of husbands," I say.

Old Mother pinches me by twisting the anklet tight. "Do you think of a husband too, foolish child? Heh! What can a husband give you? Not the finest lodge, as Raven Keeper has. Not the finest meat and corn, as she is given." She finishes the new knot and pushes my foot away. "Clean the dirt from your moccasins. Then weave, and weave straight, if you can."

"Yes, Mother."

"Tonight you bake corncakes. Better cakes than last time, I hope."

"Yes, Mother."

"And you must learn to sing her song." My mother's black eyes flash. "How much longer must I wait for you to be good enough to take her place?"

I shiver with the memory of Raven Keeper's mournful cry. "But what if she does not want to leave?"

The question earns me a hard rap across my knees with a

switch Old Mother keeps for that purpose. I gasp, but do not cry out. Old Mother pretends to be feeble because she does not enjoy work in the fields, but the welts on my knees prove she has the strength of a bear. I swallow the pain and use the energy of my rage to clean moccasins, weave baskets in straight lines, and pound dried corn into meal.

Grandmother Moon shows her full face and whispers to the village that it is time to plant. Soon she will make way for Grandfather Sun, but her milky wash on the carpet of brown leaves outside the cave is all I need for now. I do not venture very far inside—the first chamber serves my purpose well enough.

I stand in the damp gloom and practice the raven call. The notes I know by heart—up, up, and down—like a pattern repeated in the weave of a basket. I whisper the sounds over and over. The repetition is both comforting and exhilarating.

A chipmunk sits motionless on its haunches at the opening of the cave, watching me. The moonlight behind paints it black. I whisper to the chipmunk, "Craw-cree-craw-cree-craw-craw." It does not move.

I fill my chest with the close air of the cave and when I release the breath, I allow my whole throat to take over the sound. With eyes closed, I sing to the ravens. "Craw-cree-craw-cree-craw-craw!" I finish the song and let its echo ring in my ears.

When I open my eyes, the chipmunk is gone.

I bounce on my toes as I walk through the woods. I have never before sung as I have sung tonight. Perhaps I could call the ravens. How glorious it would be to stand on the hill, as Raven Keeper does, and raise my arms to the dawn! But I should not think so much of my small success. I am nothing—it is Raven Keeper who is holy.

As long as Raven Keeper sends her ravens with gifts for Man Who Is Raven every evening, the crops are not ruined by insects or taken by birds, the woods remain full of game, and fish fill the river. I do not know how this is so, or why Raven Keeper lives in loneliness on the hill. I have heard the ravens are her sons, but I am not invited into story circles and have heard no more than that.

I wonder what I always wonder. How could my mother have such hopes for me? It is her desire to live in Raven Keeper's lodge, to enjoy the reverence and offerings of the village and the benefit of my labor. But how can she be sure that the ravens will come when I call? And how will she convince Raven Keeper to give up her hill? I pause by a white birch and shiver. Does Old Mother have enough magic to harm Raven Keeper? Might she hurt her—would she kill? Paralyzed by this recurring fear, I stare into the moonlit woods.

Two points of white distract me. Two eyes reflect Grandmother Moon. Slowly I distinguish the shadow of an animal. A mountain lion. It stares at me, its head low, its haunches raised. I wrap my hand around the branch of the birch tree and squeeze it tight. The mountain lion creeps forward, never surrendering its stare.

Sweat chills my skin.

The lion snarls. Its pointed teeth glimmer yellow. I imagine those teeth clamped around my neck.

Its muscles rippling, the lion moves closer.

I have only one skill, only one strength, newfound. I fill my chest with air, tighten my throat, and scream the call of the raven. "Craw-cree-craw-cree-craw-craw!"

The sound of my cry, like a power released, invades my head and pushes out against my skull. The edges of my vision blur. "Craw-cree-craw-cree-craw-craw!"

My breath escapes me. My vision closes. In my haze, all I

can see is the double reflection of Grandmother Moon. And then I see nothing at all.

I open my eyes to morning dampness and inhale the rot of wet leaves. By my head, a chipmunk turns an acorn in its paws. *Ah, not so afraid of me now.* I check my fingers, my toes, my limbs. All there. Nothing wet with blood. Nothing missing. I stand up with the ache of stiff bones and shake with the cold. After a few faltering steps, I make my way to Old Mother's hut.

She grins when I enter. "*Aye-kye*, what took you so long?"

I had expected anger and a raised switch. Old Mother's smile confuses me.

She shuffles around the fire in a crooked dance. "Heh, heh, we are ready," she sings. "We are ready. We are ready. Heh, heh, we are ready."

I find my voice. "Ready?"

"Ah, you are modest. What a good mother I have been to make you so. I heard you before the dawn. I heard you call the ravens, Beetle Girl. Heh, heh, we are ready!"

My skin tightens.

Old Mother cackles. "Where have you been, lazy one? Celebrating in the woods?"

"No, Mother." I swallow hard. "I did not call the ravens. Perhaps it was Raven Keeper you heard. Or the ravens themselves. I ... I slept in the woods. I heard nothing. Were you worried? I am sorry if you worried."

Old Mother stops her shuffle dance around the fire. She looks up from her bent back and her eyes narrow. "You ... you ungrateful fool. You called the ravens in the woods." Her voice rumbles with anger. "And you will call them for me when we live on the hill."

My mother reaches for the polished switch.

I wake in time for the first planting. The sting of my back is fresh, but the pain in my heart, like droplets of maple sap in the snow, has hardened. No more. No more, I think. The idea for my escape had sprouted in the night and by dawn it had blossomed into a plan.

The sound of Old Mother sucking her hand in her sleep makes me cringe. What a relief it is to emerge from the rank closeness of our hut!

Across rolling fields, clusters of women stoop to caress and tame the brown earth, their bare backs awash in the yellow liquid of morning light. Young and old, they are strong and beautiful. Before I join them, I tie a rough-edged deer hide across my shoulders to hide the welts made by my mother. My heart chokes at the memory of the blows. Children of this village would never see a hand raised to them. Only Old Mother, in the darkness of our little hut, inflicts such pain and humiliation.

Little Foot's mother hands me the basket of fish and I see the women around her smile and turn away. I know their joke. They think I am proud and they would like me to smell of fish. I think to cry out and expose the evidence of my torture. *This*, I scream inside my head, *this is what makes me afraid to speak to you!* But I swing the strap around my shoulders and say nothing. I do not mind the smell of fish.

Dancing Otter, the wife of Gray Wolf, stamps the black, pointed end of a digging-pole into the ground. I follow and drop two little fish into each crater she makes. Gray Wolf's daughter, Bright Star, throws four kernels of corn and two beans into one hole, then three seeds of squash into the next. We continue this way until one row is planted and then another. The women talk and laugh and sing songs, happy for the promise of a good harvest.

This is the second planting season I have worked in the fields. Now that I labor among the women, I am entitled to a greater share of the harvest—a welcome addition to the meager provisions my mother earns for her potions and cures.

At midday we rest in the shade of the woods that edge the field. The others drink water from gourds and eat the food they had left the little children to guard. A group of hunters saunter by. Gray Wolf's son, Two Feathers, pauses to tease and smile at the little boys who beg to accompany them. As always, a pair of white-tipped turkey feathers dangle from the straight hair that falls free across his shoulders. I admire his ease and humor among the children.

Little Foot, I see, studies him too. When she feels my eyes on her, she tosses a small smoked fish at me and laughs. "Today you are Fish Girl."

I turn away, boiling with a mixture of anger and shame—Little Foot must have seen that I have no food of my own—but I slip the blackened fish into the pouch at my waist. The smoked fish will keep for days and I must hoard food for my journey.

We return to the fields and I follow Dancing Otter once again, lining her craters with dead-eyed fish. We labor in this way until Grandfather Sun makes our shadows long toward Spirit Mountain.

Little Foot's mother takes her fish basket from me. "You work well, Beetle Girl."

I am not used to praise. While I think of what reply I should give, she turns away and walks toward the village. Little Foot joins her. They swing empty baskets and sing together.

I enter my smoky hut. Without a word, Old Mother hands me a strip of dried meat.

Is this plan of flight another daydream, or will I act

tomorrow? Fear grips my body and leaves no room for hunger. But I force myself to chew the toughened flesh. I will need the nourishment.

It is usual for me to rouse before the sun, but my mother first opens an eye as I roll up my skins. She warns me in half-sleep: "Do not be late."

I emerge from the lodge into the predawn chill and find the elm that hides my buckskin sack and rolled sleeping-skin. Inside the long-handled sack is a rod and dry softwood for making fire, a flint knife, and two flat cakes of cornmeal. I loop the broad strap across my body, balance the rolled deerskin on my shoulder and walk into the woods. I move in the direction of Raven Keeper's hill in case Old Mother listens, but after a way, I turn toward a hunting path I know.

My heart races with the risk of my deceit. It has taken me two days to prepare for my escape—two days as the welts on my back healed. I feel them now, when the motion of my pack tugs the strap across my back.

I step onto the hunting path and walk north. Perhaps I will find another village. Perhaps I will die in the woods. I cannot know what lies ahead. The certainty of my course is determined only by what I leave behind.

Clouds hide Grandfather Sun, but the air has warmed. My moccasins pat the soft earth of the path. At midday, I squat at a small rocky stream and take sips of water. Two deer tiptoe to the brook and share a drink with me. I listen to the tinkling song of the water and watch the brown-eyed deer. The pleasure of the moment seeps into my skin and warms my bones.

The patter of rain begins at dusk and I unroll my deerskin at the base of a tall pine. The warm scent comforts me and the dense branches above my head provide some protection from the shower. In a circle of stones, I cover the softwood with brown pine needles, insert the hardwood rod, and twirl it between my palms. The softwood smokes and the pine needles smolder. I add a pinecone and dry twigs and soon my fire glows red and orange.

With my flint knife, I skin the fish that has been hiding in my pouch, and offer silent thanks to Little Foot.

The strap on my ankle has become uncomfortable and I blame the dampness.

I gather the skin and bones of the fish, place them in the blackness outside my small circle of light and lie down on the deerskin. I shift the anklet once again before I huddle into a restless slumber.

A dream disturbs my sleep.

I see Raven Keeper lifting her arms to the ravens at dawn. Slowly she turns her elegant face to me and smiles. Raven Keeper reaches her arms, beckoning me and my spirit soars at her welcome. I jump up and run to her, but as I am about to touch her fingertips, my leg is wrenched back and I fall to the ground. Behind me, a black bear grips the end of a long cord in its teeth. The trail of the cord leads to the leather band around my ankle. I try to tug it loose, but band and cord are fastened tight. The face of the black bear transforms into Old Mother's face and the round of its back becomes hers. With wild, laughing eyes, Old Mother slides the cord from her teeth and clenches my tether in her bony fist. She dances her shuffle dance around me while I lie helpless on the ground. *Heh, heh, we are ready. We are ready. We are ready!*

I wake with a start. The fire has died and the blackness is so complete that I do not know at first if my eyes are open. My foot throbs with pain. I touch Old Mother's leather loop and feel it tight around my ankle. Too tight. I cannot pull it looser. I fumble for the tree trunk, locate my pack, and grope inside. I wrap my fingers around the handle of my flint knife and carry its sharp edge to the anklet. I rub the leather with the blade, back and forth, back and forth. The pain goads me, even though the cloud of my mind knows this effort is futile.

The throbbing intensifies. Frustrated, I push harder. The knife snaps and a sharp pain bites my foot. My fingers feel the knife tip, embedded between the bones along the crest of my foot. I extract the flint with a swallowed scream and press my hand against the warm dribble of my blood.

"I curse you, Old Mother!"

The darkness mocks my cry. My mother's magic clutches me, keeps me prisoner. I am the fool she thinks I am, to think I could be free.

Great sobs consume me. I am determined to die here, to bear the pain until my foot shrivels and the pine needles have soaked up all my blood. If I am dead, my mother has no hope of stealing Raven Keeper's lodge. If I am dead, my mother cannot hurt me.

Time slows in the blackness of a clouded night. I measure it in countless heartbeats, each heartbeat a thud of pain.

The rain stops and a shroud of silence cloaks the forest. My still-tender back rests against the tree and I have propped my ankle upon the rolled deerskin. I do not close my eyes for the pain in my foot and the sadness in my heart.

A whisper touches my darkness. It is Raven Keeper's call. Her voice is small and distant, but the rhythm of her song and the coming of the dawn kindle a tiny flame within me. I shift the bulk that swells inside my bloodstained moccasin. My foot is the red of crushed raspberries and the wound oozes blood. There is no relief from the throbbing pain.

But I am not brave enough to stay here and die.

I find a forked branch I can use as a crutch, then gather my belongings and hobble along the hunter's path, one painful step after another, back toward the village. The going is slow and I stop many times to rest. By the time I reach Old Mother's lodge, darkness has long since fallen, and I am aware of little beyond the high-pitched screaming of crickets that vibrates inside my head.

I crawl into the lodge and curl up on a mat, panting with pain.

"Foolish ingrate," growls Old Mother. She presses her fingers into the noose around my ankle and closes her eyes.

The release stings with the bite of a knife.

I whimper like a wounded dog until I fall asleep.

With my sleeping skins rolled and balanced over my shoulder, I climb the sacred path to Raven Keeper's hill. Grandmother Moon has been turning away these past six nights. I feel her disdain as she hides her face, and find my way by the light of the stars.

My mother left me the evening of my return, but the pleasure of her absence was dampened by pain and worry. She had gone to Raven Keeper's lodge with instructions that I join her there after the sixth sun set. Thoughts of what she might do there twisted my heart.

For two suns I could not do much but throw twigs on the hot ashes of the fire pit and apply Old Mother's herb paste to my wound. Now I hobble in a stretched and bloodstained moccasin. I had broken my own flint knife against the anklet and it remains beyond repair. Old Mother owns our only remaining knife—the knife of bone forbidden to me—but would not cut me a new shoe before she left.

I pause at the rotting log that marks the opening to the thicket that had hidden me so many times. The dark shape of Raven Keeper's lodge stretches before me. Its length hints at two fire pits within, enough space to shelter more than one family, but a single line of smoke breaks the darkness above it.

I limp to the doorway and press my hand against the rough bark. After all these years spying from a distance, the closeness of the dwelling is almost unreal to me. Old Mother has instructed me to come at this time and enter. I wedge my fingers in the door, pull it open, and bow my head into the entrance.

It is not the sweet smell of Raven Keeper's herbs and stews that greets me, but the sourness of Old Mother. My wrinkled mother stands by a fire that crackles in the first circle of stones. Her teeth gleam inside a crooked grin. "Close the door, sly one. Are you waiting for a raccoon to follow you in?"

Although I had expected her to be here, Old Mother's presence in Raven Keeper's home has the shock of worms on meat.

I strain for a glimpse of Raven Keeper as I enter. The lodge is large enough for raised platforms, built the length of the walls on either side. Curved saplings make the arches that frame the ceiling. Fringed sacks and tools hang from the cross-poles and bunches of dried corncobs, their husks braided together, dangle from above. Beyond my mother, a second group of fire stones ring a pile of cold ashes, and in the shadows of the far corner is a curious circle of leaves and twigs, like a large nest.

With no sign of Raven Keeper, my emotions whirl. Should I grieve the absence of her living form—or celebrate the absence of her lifeless body?

Old Mother taunts me. "Looking for something?"

Her words are like lightning on dry wood. They ignite a flame of hatred in my heart that burns high and hot. I want to kill her. I want to cut her throat and watch the blood pool around her until she drowns in it. Through my rage, all I can croak is "Where?"

She glares at me with black eyes. "Save your fury for the dawn." She sits on a reed mat. "Not dead, if that is what you mean. Not yet, at least. She has taken a journey, heh, heh, but I am afraid she will never return."

Anger forms a scream at the base of my throat. I press the

rolled skins to my face and take many stunted breaths before I can stifle it.

"Enough," says Old Mother. "Find a place to rest."

I wipe away the silent stream from my nose and my eyes. I see my mother's bedding to the left and so choose a bench on the right. At least in this lodge I do not have to sleep as close to Old Mother's snoring stink. I curl up on the bench, one skin under and one skin over, and face the wall. I concentrate on a loose seam, where a gap in the bark breathes night air on my face.

Old Mother eats. I hear the wooden thump of spoon and bowl and the cluck of her tongue. She speaks to me.

Heh, heh!

You should have seen her. Seen the pity in her eyes the first night I came here. With a stick I came, for walking.

"Please help an old woman," said I.

She pitied me. Took me in and fed me. Though I was no relation, she laid me down on furs and called me Grandmother. Heh! The next day and the next, she fed me and bathed me. Meals as I never had! Leisure as I never dreamed! Ah, the feeble woman was an easy part for me to play! Each day I thanked her, praised her, called her Granddaughter. She grew to love me a little, I think. Love me as you never did, Beetle Girl, even though I have done so much for you. Heh, heh, perhaps she would have cared for me this way for all my days. Perhaps not. It did not matter, because I knew you would walk into this lodge after the sixth sun set. You have learned to do as I bid, at least.

So I carried out my plan. This morning, I pretended to sleep while she called the ravens. When she entered the lodge, I screamed. She came to me, the soft one, and kissed my brow and rubbed my hair. "Do not fret, Grandmother. Tell me your trouble."

I told her I had a dream I was too frightened to tell.

"Tell me," said she, with her voice full of sugar syrup. "Tell me,

Grandmother, and I will tell you what it means."

"What can it mean?" said I. "I climbed the mountain. It was a hard climb, but I was young in the dream, and strong. I came to a meadow and heard a noise. In a clump of blossoms the color of sunset, I found a crying child. This child was naked but for a flap of buckskin, and the hair—feathers for hair, black as the night. The child said to me, 'I cry for my mother. She must find me or I will die.'"

What a lie I told! What a glorious lie, this dream I invented! Complete with the crying little babe. I knew of her loss, you see, but I will not tell you how I knew. No, I will not tell you. But I will tell you this. My invention, this lie—it worked. Oh, how it worked! Raven Keeper collapsed into a heap of tears and moaning. It made me sick, how long she sputtered. Finally, she spoke.

"That is my child you saw on the mountain. My child I thought long dead."

"Thought?" said I.

"Taken from me," said she.

"You think, then," I replied slyly, "this child might be alive somewhere?"

She stopped her blubbering then and wiped her face. "That is what I believe."

"And what will you do, Granddaughter?"

"What can I do?" said she. "If I do not call the ravens, the village will suffer."

"Suffer? Can their suffering be worse than that of a mother whose child has been torn from her breast? I do not know many who can put aside a mother's love, but perhaps you can."

She turned her head to hide the tear but I saw it. Heh, heh I saw the tear and so I continued. "The people of the village do not care about your pain, Granddaughter. Why do you care about theirs?"

Raven Keeper stood tall above me, then. "You are right, Grandmother," said she. "I will go to Spirit Mountain and find the *flowers that are the color of sunset. I will find my child, missing all these years."*

Heh, heh, I watched her pack! Watched her pack and handed her a bowl of corn gruel before she left! And her gruel had a little extra something in it, a little extra something from me. She will go far, but she will never come back. Heh, heh, never come back!

"A boy or a girl?" I whisper.

Old Mother's slurping tongue grows silent for many moments. "What?"

"Raven Keeper's missing child," I say without turning. "A son or a daughter?"

The fire cracks and whistles. I hear Old Mother gather phlegm in her throat and spit it to the ground. "A son," she says.

I fall asleep with visions of a little boy in whispering grasses, the sheen on his skin the color of sunset, the wildflowers wet with his tears.

My mother shakes me. "Time to rise, fire heart."

I open my eyes and think I lie in the dim light of the village hut I had shared with my mother. The image of the flawed bark seam reminds me I lie in Raven Keeper's lodge. It reminds me that Raven Keeper is poisoned and travels alone on a false mission. Perhaps she is dead already. My head and my heart ache. I pull the sleeping skin over my face. "Let me be."

Old Mother shakes me again. "*Aye-kye*! Move from that bench. It is time to call the ravens."

I sit up with a start. My heart pounds and sweat forms under my arms and on my brow.

"There," says Old Mother. "That is better. Now prepare yourself."

"I cannot. I cannot, Mother. They will not come for me. My voice is not strong enough."

Old Mother hands me a turtle shell, sloshing with water. "You are ready. It is time."

I stand with the bowl, not moving.

"Call the ravens," says my mother. "Call them, or Man Who Is Raven will send the birds to eat the crops. He will urge the fish from the river and the deer from the forest. Call them, or the village will starve. But before the people die with swollen bellies, they will find you. They will peel your skin and grind your bones. They will blame you, Beetle Girl, because you are now the keeper of the ravens, and only you can appease Man Who Is Raven."

I bring the turtle shell to my lips with shaking hands. The bowl knocks my teeth and water drips down my chin. The liquid sticks to the dryness of my throat and I choke. Old Mother's jagged tongue speaks the truth. I must call the ravens.

My braid sways as I stoop through the doorway and I think of Raven Keeper, and how I had watched her emerge from the lodge in this manner so many times.

With a shudder, I face the dark outline of Spirit Mountain. Shorn of the crisscross branches of my customary hiding place, I feel naked and small on the hilltop clearing.

I have seen the dawn break for Raven Keeper in every season. I have seen the first yellow shafts of morning break over rolling hills wilted in the heat of summer, painted with the brilliance of autumn, and covered in winter white. Today, over the lush greenness of spring, the dawn breaks for me.

I close my eyes. In my mind, I form the image of the mountain lion. The reflection of Grandmother Moon flashes in its eyes and I feel again the power of the lion's hungry gaze. The rhythm comes to me then, like a drumbeat in my head. I relax my throat and take a breath. The first sound is a croak that startles me. I close my eyes again and sink into the presence of the lion. My heart pounds as I fill my chest with air.

"Craw-cree ..." I start again. "Craw-cree-craw-cree-craw-craw!"

I have done it!

"Craw-cree-craw-cree-craw-craw!" I open my eyes to the mountain and wait.

No motion disturbs the white peak. No black dots signal the coming of the ravens. The time for them to fly has come and gone.

I cover my face with my hands and shiver in the clearing. I have failed.

The wind carries a faraway sound that mocks me. "Craw!"

Again, the tiny sound floats to my ears. "Craw!"

I see them then, black spots, floating around each other like leaves in the wind. I count them as they soar closer. Six. My six ravens. I lift my arms with joy. Grandfather Sun warms my face and tears stream down my cheeks.

The ravens fly closer. They loom large, with wings as broad as my outstretched arms. Their black feathers glimmer purple and blue. The ravens circle above me, chattering a language of croaks and caws I do not understand. They are close enough for me to hear the wind rustling through their feathers, but they do not swoop down to me or brush my fingertips as they did with Raven Keeper. They are here, though, these six ravens, and they settle into the trees around the clearing.

I hear the cackle of Old Mother inside the lodge behind me. "Heh, heh, she has done it. She has done it. She has done it. Heh, heh, she has done it!"

I step to the edge of the hill, where an embedded boulder makes a small cliff. Below me, the village moves in a jumbled rhythm of work and play. I release my braid and shake loose my hair. The wind whips my tresses behind me and I enjoy the gentle tugging at my scalp. I lift my chin and raise my arms to my sides, straining to absorb the freedom of the moving air.

I close my eyes and lean forward. The west wind supports me. I lean farther, still supported. Only my bare toes touch the rim of the rock.

I open my eyes and find I have leaned too far. I gasp with fright ... and fall. Headfirst, with arms stretched, I fall. The drum of my heart beats faster as I watch the earth race toward me. When my head is so close to the dirt that the musty scent of earth fills my nostrils, I glide in an arc, up from the ground. My toes brush dried leaves.

I gaze from one wingtip to the other, in awe of the glossy black span of my wings. I stretch them wide and lift my beak into the wind. My heart beats quick and steady and I allow myself to breathe the experience, to inhale this new and unfettered feeling, this sensation of flight. I am free, and no longer afraid.

My feathers flutter gently as I push my wings through the air. I ease into a long glide and hear nothing but the calm whistle of the wind. I flap and glide again and again, down to the village. I look past my black beak to the earth and watch the bird-silhouette of my shadow graze along the ground, bumping over lodges and gardens and smoking racks of fish.

Each lodge puffs a feather of smoke that curves east with the wind and I make a game of weaving between them. A little boy looks up and aims a toy arrow at me. Others glance my way, but they are not frightened. I am a part of the sky and the earth and the village.

I coast above the hollow shell that is the hut I once shared with my mother. Two sticks wedge a square of bark across the opening, just as I left it, less than a moon ago. I swoop low over the planting fields, covered in the green down of new growth, but I am suddenly tired and make a wide arc, back toward the hill.

With the breeze at my back, I must flap more often to maintain my height. By the time I turn my wings upward to break the flow of air around them, and brush my claws to a stop along the boulder on the hill, I am weary.

I close my eyes for a moment and drink a final sip of happiness. When I open them, I am lying in the shadows of Raven Keeper's lodge. My bed is softer now, padded with corn husks and covered with supple skins.

I have had this dream of flight every night since I called the ravens.

With a warm breeze at my back, I carry water from the hillside spring to the fire I tend outside the lodge. My foot has healed, although a scarlet depression remains beneath the anklet. I tip the bark container and pour the clear liquid into a clay pot of coarsely ground dried corn. With wooden tongs, I pinch a red-hot stone from the flames, dip it in water, then drop it into the pot. The water sizzles and boils, and in a few moments, the corn softens. I add a ball of maple sugar to sweeten the gruel.

I speak to Raven Keeper in my mind, although I do not feel her spirit beside me. I laugh and tell her I am not used to working with such abundance. I ask her which is the third herb I have seen her add to fish stew, but I do not expect an answer. I hope she has found peace in the Land of the Dead, and relief from her loneliness.

Old Mother bangs open the door of the lodge and emerges from the smoky darkness. "The Strawberry Moon is sweet."

I stir the gruel and do not raise my eyes to her. The days are long and spent preparing. When the ravens have gone at dusk, each with a token of my labor, I am satisfied with my work, and tired. Last night, I welcomed the full face of Grandmother Moon, but did not think what it meant.

Old Mother rubs her hands together. "They come today."

With this reminder, my morning hunger vanishes. I hand Old Mother a wooden bowl with gruel and duck into the lodge to ready myself. I have not seen another person, but for my mother, in more than a dozen suns—and on this day, for the first time, the people of the village will know that it is Beetle Girl who keeps the ravens.

They arrive at the peak of Grandfather Sun's journey across the sky. Gray Wolf, with face painted red, and bands of red around his elbows, wrists, knees, and ankles, leads six from the village. He wears the lifeless head of his namesake on top of his own and the wolf's hollow pelt drapes his back. The animal's fur is coarse and dense, the color of moonlight.

Behind Gray Wolf is his son, Two Feathers, who wears slanted lines of the same red paint on his bare chest. He carries two fresh-killed rabbits in one hand and a bow in the other. Five women follow, each with a strap taut across her forehead, leaning against the weight of the basket on her back.

My ravens like to chatter all day as I work. One likes to tease me, and I must keep him from stealing the fish. Most of the day they play games in the sky above me, hunt the woods for small animals, take short journeys, or rest on branches. But with the approach of strangers, the ravens retreat to the treetops, and for once, are quiet.

I stand where Old Mother has instructed me to—in the clearing, with my back to Spirit Mountain. I wear a fine skirt of Raven Keeper's that I had found rolled in a basket beneath the bench where I sleep. It is cut from the white hide of a doe— whiter than I have ever seen—softer than I have ever felt. Across the front, black porcupine quills are embroidered in the wedged shape of a raven's tail. There is a matching tunic, embellished with shining raven wings, but on a day that is almost summer there is no need for it. Necklaces of smooth shells and bones hang between my breasts. My hair is greased and plaited and I have tied a band, painted with the black curves of raven wings, across my forehead.

I had dressed as if I were dressing another, as if playing a game of pretend. Now, as I stand before these seven villagers, the clothes and adornments meld with my body and become mine. Do they see what I feel? Will they know me as the keeper of the ravens?

Gray Wolf halts when he sees me, his jaw rigid and his eyes alert. He expects none but Raven Keeper on this sacred hill.

Two Feathers drops the rabbits and loads his bow. His arrow is pointed at my heart, but his face is not that of a hunter ready for the kill. Two Feathers' face is that of a boy who has looked twice at a beetle and seen it grow wings.

Old Mother steps from behind the lodge and speaks to Gray Wolf's feet. Her stooped posture gives her a look of exaggerated deference. "Haste would be unwise."

Gray Wolf motions to Two Feathers to lower his bow and they both walk to my fire pit, the son a step behind the father. The women drop their baskets in the shade of the trees and wait. I recognize Gray Wolf's wife, Dancing Otter, among them.

They steal silent glances, but except for Dancing Otter, none will look long at me.

Old Mother shuffles to the men. Across the fire, she says, "I had a vision of Raven Keeper's death. We came at once to an empty lodge and the dawn approached with no sign of her. I am old and my skills dwindle, but with much effort, I gave this girl the voice of a raven."

Her lie pricks me and it is only with the force of my will that I do not shout out.

"Beetle Girl has kept the ravens since before the Night Without a Moon," says Old Mother. "You have heard her at the dawn, I am sure. She calls them and they come. She prepares fine food and skins and the ravens deliver these at dusk to Man Who Is Raven." Old Mother looks up by tilting her head. "Fish fill the river. Deer roam the forest. Corn and beans and squash grow in the fields." She lifts a bony hand to the women. "Your baskets are full."

Grandfather Sun burns my scalp and brings sweat to my brow. Gray Wolf stands for a long time by the fire, his mouth set in a line of suspicion.

Without a word, Gray Wolf walks to me. I smell the paint on his face and the grease on his skin. I drop my head and he says, "Look up!" He is tall and I must lift my chin to find his eyes. They are hard and sharp, but I hold his gaze.

Gray Wolf breaks our meeting with a blink of his eyes. He turns and walks past me, to the edge of the hill, and raises his arms. "Great Father, who created all things, we stand on this hill, first of all, in praise of You."

Mosquitoes buzz about my ears. My muscles remain taut and still.

"Without the plants and the animals," says Gray Wolf, "we would be nothing, and we thank you for these. For the light and the dark, the sun and the moon, we thank you. The people of the earth live in the Great Mystery. We toil and we rest. We grieve and we celebrate. That is the way it is. That is the way of the people, the way of the animals, the way of the rocks and trees. And it is the way of the one who lives on Spirit Mountain, the one called Man Who Is Raven, to remind us of our fragile existence on this earth. The people respect Man Who Is Raven, this Spirit Bird, who has the power to direct the scavenging birds to our crops. We bow our heads and leave offerings such as we can, and give our thanks also to Man Who Is Raven, so he will think well of us, and let us live and work, so that we may feed our children in the winter." Gray Wolf lowers his hands and chants a song about the worth of the harvest, the goodness of the hunting, and his reverence for the one who calls the ravens. Two Feathers and the women place the offerings in a circle around him as he sings.

So that we may feed our children in the winter. The weight of Gray Wolf's words lie heavy on my shoulders.

Gray Wolf is the last to leave. He pauses before me, but does not turn his face, and I study the straight lines of his painted profile as he speaks. "The hill is yours," he says. "Do not defile it. Do not leave it."

When they are gone, I drop to my knees and hug my arms around my body. The trembling does not end until the shadow of the lodge creeps toward me.

There is still much to do and I rouse myself. I store most of the goods left for me. The rabbits I skin with a flint knife that had belonged to Raven Keeper, and boil their meat in a stew. I save the fur for a coat I am making for Man Who Is Raven, but keep some for myself. I will use it to fashion a new pouch to wear at my waist.

At dusk, long shadows darken the clearing, and I line six small vessels along its edge. One by one, the ravens swoop down from the trees. The first two grab bark containers, steaming with rabbit stew. The next two sweep up crisp corncakes in reed baskets. The fifth clutches the wooden handle of a basket filled with the first of the wild strawberries. For the sixth, my trickster, there is a sack of smoked fish.

The ravens fly into the fading light and by the time they reach the next hill, they are gone into the darkness.

The Spirit of the Wind smoothes my feathers with a caress of gentle power. I gather his strength beneath my wings and climb. When the lodges are anthills below me, I release the curl of my wings and fall into a breathless dive. East, south, west, and north—they were never enough. Earthward and skyward add a new dimension of freedom and happiness—six directions are mine to conquer.

Through eyes made moist by streaming air, I see the treetops as a wash of green. Left I swoop, then right, swinging in lazy curves above the village.

The Three Sisters—corn, beans, and squash—display their riches in the fields ahead. I glide in close and let my talons brush the soft tips of the cornstalks. A young girl pulling weeds jumps up and waves me away. She fears I will steal the precious yield. How can she know it is Beetle Girl who casts a fleeting shadow along the field? How can she understand that I hunger only to protect this crop?

The people of the village have already danced with the taste of summer squash and green corn. Soon the Harvest Moon will smile and worries of a hungry winter will be buried deep in storage pits.

Farther north, a dense expanse of pine trees beckons me. My body yearns to explore beyond the village, but I resist. If I fly too far I might not wake in time to call the ravens. I tilt the span of my wings, make an arc about an invisible point at my wingtip, and turn back toward my lonely hill.

My return is interrupted by an unusual sight—smoke curls above the village hut I once shared with Old Mother. The bark square I had wedged against the doorway is gone. It is the custom for a lodge to be left undisturbed when closed in this manner. And who would risk bad magic that may have been left by my mother? I circle the hut, hoping the tenant will emerge, but the lodge remains still, and furtive glances through the smoke-hole reveal nothing but shadows.

A crack of thunder shatters the vision, leaving me in utter blackness. Am I Raven or am I Beetle Girl? The answer is the hollow patter of rain on the bark roof.

Why must you wake me, mighty Storm Bird? It is Raven I wish to be. As Raven, I serve the Spirit of the Wind. As Beetle Girl, I serve a murdering witch.

I lie in the sweltering closeness of the lodge, uncovered. My limbs seem absent, as if still caught in the dream, and I have no desire to call them back. The six ravens of the sunrise bring me peace, but these dreams—these dreams are the only joy I know.

As the cornstalks sprouted and grew tall, so have I dreamt it. As the little children picked the thicket clean of wild berries, so have I dreamt it. As the boys and girls ran races and played their games with sticks and balls, so have I dreamt it. Across the waxing, waning moons of summer, as I soared and slipped above the rhythmic phases of village life, so have I dreamt it.

But in this night's dream, someone burns a fire in the hut, someone unknown. Like the incessant heat of the lodge, this mystery disturbs me.

Thunder claps with another great flap of Storm Bird's wings. A flash of lightning outlines the square edges of the doorway and illuminates the puddle beneath it. Then, as if by this signal, the rain ends. All is quiet but for the whisper of rustling leaves.

I step out to a damp, darkened world of dripping leaves and

muddy puddles, shake the lowest branch of a young oak, and let the droplets cool my face. I slide my bare feet along the wet grass of the clearing and walk toward the dawn.

I no longer chant my morning song with trepidation. When I sing, the ravens come. When I sing, the song renews me.

"Craw-cree-craw-cree-craw-craw!"

Through a blanket the color of wet ashes, Grandfather Sun burns a hint of white radiance.

"Craw-cree-craw-cree-craw-craw!"

My ravens break the mist, all at once, like the waves of black paint that decorate my headband.

They come to me as always, never out of order, and never any closer. Always First leads his brothers in a ring around me. Proud Beak follows, with breast feathers ruffled and eyes wide. Six ravens pass before my outstretched arms, from left to right. Always First breaks the circle and swoops into the woods. Proud Beak makes an acrobatic turn and follows.

Observes From Trees finds his perch, never the same one twice. Restless Lookout flies high and makes a vigilant loop around the hill. He will return and then repeat this circular flight many times over the course of the day. Flies Too Far makes an early excursion. Perhaps he needs to escape the hot dampness more than I. He swerves toward the river, but before he is gone too long, Always First emits a long, admonishing croak, and Flies Too Far returns.

I do not see where Little Trickster has gone. He makes a game of stealing food or misplacing my tools. Sometimes, if he ruins a stew or upsets a bag of meal, it puts me in bad humor. But then he glides past me with a turn of his head and a sparkle in his eye and I am happy to forgive him.

This morning, I have a plan for Little Trickster. I splash the water away from the puddle in the lodge doorway and fill the space with loose earth from the herb garden. But before I stomp down the dirt, I wrap a handful of mud in a corn leaf and secure it with twine made from a strip of dried husk. On a bark tray that still holds the curve of the tree, I stack six identical packets—three on the bottom, then two, then one. Five contain soft chestnuts I boiled yesterday, and the sixth contains the mud. I add my fire-starting tools and a handful of dry kindling to the tray of chestnut wraps, carry it outside, and set it down on the cutting stone beside the outdoor fire pit. With the mud-filled corn leaf at the top, my joke for Little Trickster is ready.

Grandfather Sun struggles to burn the mist cradled in the valleys, but Spirit Mountain, cold and stubborn, fights the dawn. I flip the dripping mat that covers the fire pit, squat over the dry ashes, and twirl and tease the fire to life.

This is the time for my morning prayer.

I reach in the rabbit-skin pouch for a pinch of tobacco and sprinkle it on the growing flames. I give thanks to Great Spirit, Grandfather Sun, Grandmother Moon, Mother Earth, and Man Who Is Raven. Most others who honor their ancestors have known grandparents, and even great-grandparents. They have lived among them and watched them grow old. I acknowledge faceless ancestors and generations unknown.

My final prayer is for Raven Keeper and I throw a second pinch of tobacco into the flames. "Praise to you, Righteous One, Beautiful Mother, who kept the ravens before me. I thank you for your lessons of goodness and honor your spirit." With these words, the sharp claws of sorrow grip my heart. I listen to the crackle of the fire and stare at orange flames through a haze of tears. If I had been brave enough to die, Raven Keeper—elegant, lonely Raven Keeper—might walk among her ravens yet.

I let the pain carry me for a few moments. It would carry me all day if I let it, but there is work to do. I slip into the lodge and take up the basket of early corn to be parched and stored. I stomp the dirt in the entryway once more on my way out, but quickly turn and duck back inside. My joke has worked. The corn leaf filled with mud is missing and I do not want Little Trickster to see me smile.

Inside, Old Mother snorts and rises, and shuffles back to the storage room. All day, she eats. Not even three bears can eat as much as Old Mother, I think. I make no comment because the food in her belly makes her eyes heavy. Every night, she falls asleep at dusk and does not stir again until after the dawn.

I balance a long pole and push aside the bark flap that covers the smoke-hole. Old Mother emerges from the storage room with her arms full, but remains stooped in the back corner of the lodge, with her back to me. On the bench in front of her is a circle of intertwined twigs, made tight with earth and milkweed fluff. I call it a nest, but it is too large for any bird I know. When I first became keeper of the ravens, I slid my fingers along its buckskin center and tapped the ends of the twigs. I sensed its importance then, and have always treated it with reverence.

I set the basket of corn on the ground and creep toward Old Mother. Over her shoulder, by the light of the open doorway, I watch as her gnarled fingers sift a collection of nuts and berries in the well of the nest.

My cry is like a raven screech.

Old Mother leaps back and some of her mixture bounces across the floor. She whirls around and faces me with wild eyes. "*Aye-kye*, evil girl, look what you've done!" With arms flailing, she waddles to her bench. "Where is it? Where is the switch?"

My concern is for the nest. Berries have already stained the buckskin lining. "Please, Old Mother," I coo. "I didn't mean to startle you. I only thought ... I only thought the largest of the wooden bowls might suit you better."

Old Mother pauses in her search and lifts an eyebrow. "You do not want me to touch that mess of sticks, do you?"

I am reduced to the truth. "No, Old Mother."

She runs her tongue along her bottom lip. "Get the bowl and

pick up what I lost."

I fetch the bowl, transfer the mixture, and gather the stray ingredients.

Old Mother makes herself comfortable outside on a log in the clearing. When I hand her the bowl, she leans over and shovels nuts and berries into her mouth with a cupped hand. Bits of food fly from her mouth as she speaks. "Do you know why you love that jumble of twigs so much?"

This is more than a question and I answer with nervous anticipation. "No, Old Mother."

"Heh, heh, you do not. Nor will I tell you. Heh, heh! Now get to work."

My jaws are tight when I turn back to tend the fire.

"*Aye-kye!*"

I jump at Old Mother's cry and spin around. A lump of wet mud sits on her head. It drips down her forehead and into her berries. A strip of corn-husk twine dangles from her coarse hair.

Little Trickster swoops past me with eyes that sparkle and I go to my tasks with a lighter heart.

Without a sound, my moccasins tread the soft path that leads down from the sacred hill. The face of Grandmother Moon is shorn of the first brilliant roundness that summoned the harvest. She watches over the sleeping village and lights my way. Although my mission is filled with danger, the familiar path is comforting.

I had spent the last moon of summer infected with the sickness of curiosity. Who continues to burn the fire in the old hut? My dreams never showed me, and every morning I woke in a fever of frustration. I yearned to walk from the hill and see for myself, but feared the risk. Old Mother never stirred in the night, but if I were caught near the village, what would Gray Wolf do? I had waited, night after impatient night, for the last day of the Harvest Festival, when the people of the village would sleep long and well.

The woodland smells of musty sweetness. At the base of the hill, I brush the leaves of the blue spruce and the white ash as if we are old friends, reunited.

I stop at a sound, short and gruff. I keep my body still and turn my eyes and head for signs of a visitor. The trees that surround me melt into shadows. Nothing moves. I walk on, hearing only the drumbeat of my heart.

I am more careful as I creep through the woods that edge the village, and I watch the ground for twigs and pinecones. Halfway to the hut, I hear a feather of movement behind me and spin around in time to see the tail of an animal disappear behind a wide pine tree. I think it might be a dog and this thought makes my heart beat quicker. Dogs are trained for the hunt—it is the master I fear, more than the animal.

I scoff at myself. It is more likely a raccoon. But I cannot continue with this question behind me, and so I turn back to investigate. When I am close enough to touch the shadowed pine, a tall form separates from it and I jump back.

The shadow-man floats in a cloud of animal scents—sweat and bear grease and forest musk. I stand motionless as his little black dog sniffs my ankles. Finally, he takes one step toward me and his high cheekbones and proud chin are revealed in the moonlight.

It is Two Feathers.

We do not speak for a long time.

His voice is low, but he is close and every word rings clear. "I wonder why the one who calls the ravens wanders so far."

I gather courage and take a gamble. "I wonder why the son of the sachem walks upon the forbidden hill."

His silence tells me I have hit the mark. Two Feathers has been following me since the beginning of my journey. He will keep my secret, perhaps, if I keep his.

I cannot continue to the hut as I had planned, but this standoff makes me bold. "A fire burns in the last hut before the fields."

Two Feathers acknowledges this statement with a slight tilt of his head.

"It would not bring bad magic to name the person who burns this fire," I say.

Two Feathers' stare does not have the intensity of his father's. Perhaps this is because he is young—not more than eighteen winters—or perhaps because he comes to me with greater trust. Whatever his reason, he answers, "Raven Keeper lights the fire."

The incessant motion of the dog's paw as it scratches an ear seems to scatter Two Feathers' words, so that, even though they are few, I cannot completely understand them. My confusion makes the trees swim. I cover my face and squat. "Raven Keeper walks in the Land of the Dead," I say to my knees.

"Raven Keeper walks upon the earth among the living."

I struggle to hide tears of happiness as I rise on quivering legs.

His eyes narrow. "Here in the darkness, it is hard to tell relief from disappointment."

"Oh, but it is relief! Please, please tell me how it is that she lives."

He glances toward the village. "I will be missed."

"You must stay." My words have the sound of a command, although I did not mean them to.

Two Feathers lifts his chin higher, but does not leave.

I lower my head and stare at his fringed leggings, bound below each knee with a strip of hide. Two moccasins, discolored from long forest journeys, are planted firmly within the shadows on the path. "Forgive me for speaking to you this way."

The words of the young hunter hum in the darkness above my head. "Gray Wolf, my father, found her to the east, in the hills where he tracked a summer buck. At first he thought her gone to the Land of the Dead, but he saw ... he saw she clung to the Land of the Living. He made a sled and laid her on it."

I keep my head bowed and feel the whisper of his breath on my scalp.

"He pulled her back along the hunting path. He brought her into our lodge and we made a circle of healing around her. She stayed with us and my mother nursed her."

It is hard to find my voice. "And now, is she well?"

I hear Two Feathers inhale. "My father told her she must

reclaim her lodge on the hill, but she would not listen. He told her he would kill the witch, but Raven Keeper said that if he did, the witch would surely carry Sister Raven with her to the Land of the Dead. Raven Keeper begged Gray Wolf—she begged him not to let Sister Raven die."

I lift my head. "Sister Raven?"

There is softness in his dark eyes. "It is what you are called."

These are so many mysteries at once, I hardly know what to ask.

Two Feathers moves his mouth as if to say more, but steps away and disappears into the shadows. His black dog prances after him.

I cannot move. It is too much at once for my mind and my heart.

A chipmunk scurries past. It startles me from my thoughts and I race back to the hill. Up and up I climb along the path, never pausing until I come to the clearing at the top. Panting for breath, my heart pounding, I fall to my knees in the long, damp grass and raise my face and arms in soundless joy.

Raven Keeper lives!

Grandfather Sun splashes the trees and hills with red and yellow and orange, while Mother Earth paints a gentle reminder of her strength with patches forever green. With my arms heavy with firewood, I pause to watch a flock of fiery leaves twirl and dance above the clearing.

Restless Lookout finishes his loop above the hill and finds a post in the highest branches of a tall pine. The forest vibrates with the craws and croaks of an argument between Always First and Little Trickster.

I stack the wood on the side of the lodge while Proud Beak grooms his feathers on a tree limb behind me. "What is the disagreement this time?" I ask him.

Proud Beak answers, "Cree-crawk," as if to say, *The usual nonsense.*

The hills breathe the far-off echo of a victory whoop. I wonder if the triumphant hunter is Two Feathers and imagine him standing by the carcass, sprinkling tobacco and giving thanks to the Spirit of the Deer.

I inhale the sharp chill of autumn and gaze upon the patchwork hills. "There is a new name for me," I tell Proud Beak.

He does not answer, but I hear the click of preening behind me.

"I heard it once. In the time of the Harvest Moon. Would you like to know it?"

Proud Beak rumbles a soft sound.

My throat tightens with a mixture of pride and pain. "I am called ... I am ... Sister Raven."

There is more I wish to share, but Old Mother has big ears, and that is all I dare to say. Someday, perhaps, I will tell Proud Beak that Raven Keeper begged for my life.

One by one, I unroll the mats and skins I found neatly stacked in the storage alcove. I tie the mats to the inner frame of the lodge with basswood string. The wind blows cold from the north. It finds the gaps between the bark panels of the lodge, and even near the fire, I can sometimes feel its icy sting. The tightly woven mats seal the walls and their graceful designs— in red, white, yellow, and black—warm the lodge.

A section of wall above my sleeping bench remains

uncovered and I return to the storage alcove for one last mat. If there is not another, I will weave my own. But when I reach far under the bottommost shelf, my fingers touch soft deer hide.

Across my bed, I unroll a hand's width of the skin. A picture is painted there. The yellow circle is the head of a person and the yellow lines below it represent the body, arms, and legs. I unroll the hide a bit more. Beside the head is painted a black feather that makes an arc upward. At the tip of the feather are two curved lines, like eyebrows, joined at the center with a black dot. Above the black curves is the shape of an arrowhead, in red, with its tip painted white.

Old Mother grunts. "What are you staring at?" She tosses a thin log on the fire. "Winter is coming and all you do is stand about."

My heart flutters at my discovery. Without a word, I gather the skin and carry it outside. My lazy mother cowers from the cold and will not follow.

A strip of white along the north edge of the lodge is all that remains of an early snow. Leggings and long sleeves protect me from the late-autumn chill and Grandfather Sun warms my face.

On a dry portion of ground, I smooth open the roll, and the colors come alive in the sunlight—a person in yellow, a feather by the head, curved black lines, and a red arrowhead, tipped in white. The first set of images is followed by a second, identical set. Then a third, fourth, fifth, and sixth. I unroll the last bit of hide to reveal a seventh yellow figure. Its round head and sticklike body are the same as the previous six, but it stands alone, without feather or curved lines or arrowhead.

"Crok!"

I lift my head to admire the grace of Flies Too Far. With the snowy peak of Spirit Mountain behind him, he stretches his wings and glides toward our hilltop. When I look down, the images have more meaning. The black curved lines are the wings of a raven and the white-tipped arrowhead is not an arrowhead at all. It is Spirit Mountain.

I had heard that the ravens were Raven Keeper's sons, and it must be true. Here are the seven children of Raven Keeper. Six sons who became ravens and flew to Spirit Mountain. And the seventh son? He is lost. Yes. At Old Mother's prompting, Raven Keeper abandoned her hill in order to search for him. I brush my fingers across the images and feel the rough interruptions of paint across the softness. Why do your children fly as birds, Raven Keeper? And where is your seventh son?

I face the pictures to the wall when I tie the painted skin above my bed and do not secure the bottom corners. As Old Mother sleeps, I lie on my bed and lift the skin. Firelight flickers across the yellow figures as Raven Keeper's seven sons sway and dance above me.

By the light of the fire, I put the last stitch in the coat of rabbit furs. It is long and hooded and made of many rabbits—some that were offered, like the pair from Two Feathers, and some that I trapped myself. It is for Man Who Is Raven, who walks across the snowy peak of Spirit Mountain. I stand and slip the coat around my shoulders and the sleeves flop past my hands. I enjoy the weight of my creation, and its softness. It is almost an embrace.

On her bench across the fire, Old Mother snorts and sucks her hand. She still sleeps from dusk until past dawn, even though the winter nights are far longer than the days. She spends the daylight indoors, eating and complaining of the cold. I hide the logs, or she would make the fire blaze all day. But firewood is precious—some carried up the hill on the backs of the village women—and I will not have it wasted. It is warm enough inside.

Too warm, in this coat. I take my snowshoes from a peg on the sapling frame, lift the buckskin lining, and push open the door. I welcome the tingle of cold air on my face and climb up the mound of snow that surrounds the doorway. I slip my fur-lined moccasins into the snowshoes and feel the crunch and give of ice-crusted snow with each drag and step.

The icy cloud of my breath melts into the night air. My hood slips back when I look skyward and the north wind stings my ears. The full face of Grandmother Moon hovers at the treetops. Directly overhead, the seven stars of winter show off their brilliance in the speckled canopy of night. I think of the reverse—my six dots of midnight in the morning whiteness—and a feeling of grief tugs at my heart, as if, like the stars, there should be seven, and one has been missing all this time.

I look away and shake my head. Sadness creeps into my heart too easily. It eats until it has its fill and leaves nothing but a hollow ache. I do not want to know this feeling. Did sorrow gnaw at Raven Keeper's heart this way? Does she find relief within the heartbeat of the village? Dance to the drums of the Winter Festival, Raven Keeper. Dance to the drums for me!

I stumble into the lodge, throw the coat aside, and crawl into my bed. If I cannot dance, then I will fly. My dream-journeys have lengthened with the winter nights and the effort of flying is eased by the thickened air. I venture farther, fly higher. I follow the river to snow-covered landscapes I have never seen before. But always, too soon, I sense the dawn and return to my lonely life on the hill.

In the morning, I call the ravens and they fill six empty spaces in my heart.

"Stay close," I tell Flies Too Far. "It is a day of offerings."

Observes From Trees croaks low, then high.

"Yes," I say. "I can only watch, just as you do. But it makes me happy to look upon new faces." I do not tell Observes From

Trees about the face I hope to see. Two Feathers has not joined his father on this hill since the summer past, when he aimed an arrow at my heart.

At midday, Gray Wolf is the first to emerge from the sacred path. Behind him, six women, covered in the warm fur of beaver and raccoon, lean their heads against the straps of their burden-baskets. Pinched-face Little Foot is among them. When she turns, I sense a swollen belly under her furs. I wonder if she is now the wife of Two Feathers.

Sorrow gnaws with sharpened teeth.

I push my wings through chilled air and follow my shadow east along the river. Sunset paints the sky a shimmering gray and the reflection of new leaves ripples green upon the water. The springtime nights are shorter, and so my dreams are shorter too, but I fly until the very end, until the last moment before I must wake to call the ravens.

A flock of geese makes an arrow pointing north and fills the air with a barrage of squawks. Two men paddle a canoe heavy with dripping nets and gleaming fish and I sigh at the memory of the smoked fish I hid for my failed escape, almost one year ago.

I glimpse movement in the cleft between two hills and tilt my wings to circle lower. My beak parts for a small cree-cree of laughter. It is the little boy Old Mother had healed last spring. His vibrant body free of sores, he holds his little bow high and shoots practice arrows into the trees. But another sight quickens my heartbeat. A large brown bear, hungry from its winter sleep, stalks the boy.

I dive down, but my wings are wide and the forest is dense. My wingtip strikes the branch of a budding oak and I tumble until I capture the wind again. Still finding my balance, I swoop past the bear from behind and scream a loud croak in its ear.

"Crawk!"

The bear does not falter, but the boy takes heed. His hair flies from his shoulders as he whirls around and shows me his eyes, wide with fear. I clutch a low branch with my claws and place myself between the pursued and pursuer. The light has faded and the shadow of the hulking bear looms closer. With my eyes on the bear, I shout to the boy to run, and run swiftly.

"Craw-cree-cree!"

The rapid pat-pat of the boy's footsteps trail into the woods behind me.

The bear rears up, a sharp pain stings my neck, and I fall on my feathered back. The face of the bear fills my vision and its hot breath stinks of death. *Errr-grrr!* The bear's fangs glisten as it raises a paw. I flip to my belly with a clumsy, frantic flutter of my wings and take the blow upon my back. Sharp claws scrape my shoulders.

Errr Grrr!

It strikes again.

Errr Rrrr Grrr!

And again.

I shut my eyes to the pain.

Its growl increases in pitch. *Eeerrr Rrrrull Grrrull!*

Evil girl!

I open my eyes.

Old Mother stands above me with the switch raised. "Evil girl! Evil girl! You did not call them!"

I glance at the light that edges the doorway and jump from my bench. My legs, still half in the dream, crumple beneath me. I dig my fingernails into the dirt and pull my body across the floor.

Old Mother shuffles past and kicks my elbow. She swings the door open against the first stirrings of daylight. "There, you see. No ravens!"

I lean into my palms, slide my knees beneath me, and crawl through the opening.

Outside, I stagger to the edge of the clearing. It is not too late. I will call them now. I will call them and they will come. I tighten my throat and exhale into the morning mist, but my raven croak fractures into choking sobs. My mind lifts into the weightlessness of dream. I clutch my head and force cool air through my nostrils.

My first craw is a whimper and my second is not much more.

"Craw-cree."

My voice cracks. "Craw-cree."

Tears flow. "Craw-craw."

It is no use. My call is dead and I am too late. There are no black dots among the gray clouds that conceal Spirit Mountain. There are no fluttering wings. There are no squawks of welcome. My ravens are lost.

I fall to my knees and tell myself this is not happening. It is a dream and I will wake. I will wake and laugh that I have dreamt this. But the streaks of dawn are real. The frigid air is real. The grass in my fists that I have torn from the ground is real.

"No," I cry. "No! No! You must come to me. Always First, lead the way. Little Trickster, where are you?"

Before the dawn, I was the keeper of the ravens. Now I have failed. I am nothing.

I wipe the liquid that runs from my nose. Stupid, selfish girl. What about the village? As long as there was someone to call the ravens, the harvest was assured. What will Man Who Is Raven do? Will he now let loose a swarm of birds to eat the crop? Will he let the people starve?

I feel my mother's cold hand on my neck. She wraps her fingers around my braid and yanks my head back, so that I have no choice but to face her. Her eyes blaze and saliva pools in one corner of her mouth. "Worthless maggot. To think of the years I wasted with you. I should have killed you then, when you were a squirming babe in my arms." Old Mother raises her free hand, her bone knife clutched tight in her fingers.

I can hardly breathe.

"I will think of what story to tell," says my mother, "after—"

A flame of anger moves me. With two hands, I grab Old Mother's blue-veined ankle and pull with all my strength. Old Mother topples backward and lands on her back. A hard grunt of air passes her lips and the knife flies from her hand. My arms outstretched, I fling my body to the side and grab the freed weapon by its handle.

My heart is a beating drum about to burst. I turn the knife in my fingers and point the blade toward the living, breathing reason for my suffering.

Old Mother moans.

I hate this woman who calls me maggot. I hate this woman, who will not love me. How could this be my mother, who raised a knife to me—who wanted me dead?

Ha! So I am like you, after all, Mother. I want you dead.

My fingers grip the handle. My arm, raised to strike, trembles.

Do it. Do it.

Old Mother opens her eyes—they flicker with comprehension, then glisten with fear. Her lip trembles. A pile of loose skin and twisted bones, she no longer appears to be the witch I feared. How can it be that with one blink of my eyes, the monster has transformed? The creature that lies beneath me now is a pitiful old woman, crippled and powerless.

It is a trick. Sink the knife into her withered heart. Be free.

I take my freedom with one swoop of my mother's bone knife.

She gasps as it passes her face.

I guide the blade past her body, flip the knife in my hand, and slip the tip beneath the beaded leather band at my ankle. The bone blade pierces the leather and the band pops from my ankle like a snake in a leap of death.

Tears flow hot on my cheeks. I pick up the broken tether

and stand tall.

"Aye, aye," whimpers Old Mother. "My child, my own. Have pity."

I back away from her.

She raises a hand to me. "Help your old mother who loves you."

I turn and run into the lodge. There is not much time.

I fan the coat of rabbit skins across the floor and lay on top of it goods that will not perish on a journey—dried meats and fish, walnuts, balls of maple sugar. Raven Keeper's embroidered skirt and tunic that I wear on offering days lie close and I add them to the pile. I wrap the coat around all these, secure the bundle with long strips of hide, and fashion two carrying-straps. My rabbit-skin pouch holds the knife, the broken anklet, and lumped portions of cornmeal and molasses that I had baked in hot ashes.

I step into my moccasins and stoop through the lodge doorway, into the light. The muscles in my thighs tighten as I stand under the weight of the bundle on my back. New strength surges through my blood and through my bones. Is this freedom that I feel? Perhaps it is confidence—confidence in a plan I formulated the instant the leather band slipped from my ankle.

My poor, bent mother staggers toward the lodge. Her body rocks as she stamps one heavy foot after another. "Wait, my child, wait. What are you doing?" She struggles for breath. "They will come for me—for us. You must convince them you can bring the ravens again. You must take me with you. Daughter, you must take me with you."

Her words, which before would have brought me great distress, are now like the chatter of a chickadee. I sprint past her pleading hands and run down the side of the hill that faces Spirit Mountain. I slide and slip and reach my hands to the rocky ground for support. The forest closes in at the base of the hill, but I do not stop. To the village, my silence at dawn was more deafening than the loudest alarm. They will come for me. If Gray Wolf is away from the village, I will have more time.

The labor of my breathing echoes in my ears as I duck under tree limbs and plow through the brush. My breath puffs hard and steady as I run toward the rain of light through the trees.

Dusk. I have rested only once to wash my face in a beaver's pond and take rationed bites of the ashcakes. Cold and weariness wear away bits of the determination that had fueled this day's journey. As I sense the growing incline at the base of Spirit Mountain, seeds of doubt take root in my heart.

Up I climb along the path. The muscles of my legs scream and the bundle strapped across my back grows heavier with each step. A gust of freezing air stings my cheeks and announces the coming of night to the mountainside.

I feel my way along the path and scan the shadows for a sign of shelter.

An owl calls. Hoohoo-hoohoo! Hoohoo-hoohooaw!

Smoke. The scent tickles my nose, and before I can think to hide, a sudden turn in the path leads me into the glow of a tiny campfire. The shadows of the flames dance lightly on the wrinkled face of the old man who tends it. He looks up at me as if I had been expected on this small jut of level ground—as if I had just returned from gathering sticks for his fire. I stand before him, too startled to move, and he speaks to me.

"Come closer, young one, and warm yourself."

The words are almost strange—since I spoke to Two Feathers at harvest-time, I have heard only Old Mother's growl and Gray Wolf's prayers on offering days.

Thinking that I possess neither the means for my own fire nor the strength to continue farther, I kneel and thank the old man for his kindness. The warmth of the flames melts the last cold band of resolve that has driven me this far. I release the bundle from my back and a long breath escapes my throat.

The old man lifts a skewer laden with the roasted flesh of a squirrel and smiles. His cascade of snow-white hair almost conceals the beaver-skin blanket draped across his shoulders and his smoky eyes sparkle with the orange and red of the flames.

I break a lump of cornmeal and molasses for us and we share our meager meal in peaceful silence.

When we are finished, the old man speaks again. "For many, a journey may have a destination ..." He pauses so long, I am not sure he will continue. "And for many, it may not."

"I know where I go," I tell him. "To the top of this mountain."

"A mountain holds many dangers," he says. "Especially at its peak."

The comfort of this man's food and fire leaves me free, somehow, to unburden my heart. "I will call the six ravens from the top of the mountain, so that they can hear me and know I have not forgotten them. I will beg Man Who Is Raven to forgive me and to spare the village." I run my fingers across the bundle beside me—across precious offerings wrapped in a rabbit-skin coat I fashioned myself. "I have these gifts for him. And I have myself to offer too, if such a sacrifice will appease him."

The old man produces a pipe from the folds of his cloak and lifts a burning twig to light it. "Seven," he says. "There are seven ravens."

Not wanting to offend my host, I hesitate to disagree. "Forgive me, but there were six ravens that I called, and six that came, for all these moons—until this day—my day of shame." My throat sticks and I cannot say more.

The old man puffs on his pipe and stares at the fire for a long while. "I wish to tell a story," he says.

I would like very much to distract my mind from the pain of my failure—although springtime is not usually the season for stories. In the village, stories are reserved for winter, when the nights are longer and the duties of survival are less. But stories are treasures, and if I had ever considered myself poor, it was only because I was lacking in these.

I lie against the balled patchwork of rabbit skins and listen.

Of times not long past.

One day, a young maiden, who thought herself alone in a field of wildflowers, lifted her arms to an east wind, threw her head back, and let the wind carry her long hair behind her. Man Who Is Raven, who soared above the girl, deemed her more beautiful than any bird in flight. He flew to the ground and took his human form. He was a man of imposing size, with piercing eyes set slightly wide. His shining black hair flowed to his knees and many glossy black feathers were woven into it. "I want you for my wife," he told the girl.

The girl looked at the striking warrior before her. She saw the ways their hearts were alike and was at first inclined to agree, but she thought again. "My parents are old. If I go with you, there will be no one to care for them."

Raven is the northern cousin of Crow. His heart is colder and his temper fierce. He rumbled an awful cry from deep within his throat. "Cree! Craw! You must be my wife."

The girl trembled, but refused again.

Man Who Is Raven jumped into the sky. His arms became wings and he flew up and up to Spirit Mountain. There, he called upon his cousins—Crow and Grackle and Redwing—and the next day, a black cloud of birds descended on the budding fields of the village and picked clean the crop.

That evening, Man Who Is Raven came to the lodge of the girl's parents and asked if he could take her for his wife. The old parents, being kind and unselfish, and also unaware of the true identity of the handsome warrior, put the proposal in their daughter's hands. The girl understood the power of Man Who Is Raven. If she did not accept his offer, he would not allow a second crop to flourish that season, and the people of the village would starve. And so she agreed to become his wife. He carried her on his raven back and she flew with him, high into the sky.

At the top of Spirit Mountain, Man Who Is Raven and the young woman lived as husband and wife. Every day, the wife said to her husband, "My parents are old and they need me," and every day he ignored her words.

Under the Snow Blinder Moon, the wife bore a son and she set the infant in a raven's nest lined with buckskin. She said to her husband, "My parents are old and they need me." Man Who Is Raven, softened by the child, and grateful for the good attention of his wife, agreed to allow her to return to the village.

With the child in a cradleboard on her back, the wife entered her parents' lodge. They were not there, for they had already departed to the Land of the Dead. The early crop having been ruined, and the later crop of that same year having been sparse, the two old people had perished of hunger.

To ease his wife's sorrow, Man Who Is Raven made her a home on the high hill that faces Spirit Mountain. In the daylight he stayed with her as husband, but when the sun set, he became a raven and flew to his home on the mountain peak. The infant stayed with the wife on the hill, day and night, until the following winter, when Man Who Is Raven declared the child ready to join him. At dusk, the wife watched both husband and son take the form of ravens and fly away. The following dawn, the wife called them back. It was a song of rumbling croaks—a raven call her husband had taught her. And soon the loneliness the wife felt at their nightly departure was eased by the arrival of a second son, also born under the Snow Blinder Moon.

And so it was. By the seventh winter, seven children had been born to the wife. Each day at dusk, she watched her husband and six sons take the form of ravens and fly away. She was left alone with the seventh babe, who slept in the bed of sticks and earth. For six moons, she summoned her family with a raven call at dawn, and they remained for all the daylight hours in their human form. But when the Green Corn Moon shone its last rays on the lodge, before Grandfather Sun rose to look upon the earth, the wife of Man Who Is Raven found the bed of sticks and earth empty, and her seventh child gone.

The wife scoured the hill for signs of thieving animals. In the village, she overturned every basket and looked into the face of every infant. She returned to the lodge, empty-handed and heartbroken.

With a wife and family, the heart of Man Who Is Raven had thawed, but when he learned of the lost child, the layer of northern ice returned. He accused his wife of hiding the child and he accused the villagers of assisting her in the deceit. Ignoring all cries of innocence, he called upon his cousins, the scavenging birds, and they ravaged the village fields once more. Man Who Is Raven punished his wife further: When she called for her sons at dawn, six ravens would come, but six ravens they would remain. Only at night, at the top of Spirit Mountain, out of her sight and touch, would they be allowed to take their human form.

The wife performed her daily tasks in the stillness of the lodge, pining for her sons and grieving for the seventh child. Every day at dawn she summoned the six ravens, and every day at dusk she sent six ravens back to the mountaintop with baskets of cooked food and other gifts.

The people of the village now feared the wrath of Man Who Is Raven. They took corn and squash and venison to the wife's lodge at every full moon, to make sure she would continue to send gifts to appease him. The wife accepted the offerings, not because she was afraid of her husband but because she wished to provide for her children, who walked with their father on Spirit Mountain.

Day after day, year after year, the lonely woman called the

ravens. The villagers continued to bring her offerings, even when most did not remember she had been wife and mother. From that day until this, she is the woman they call Raven Keeper.

That is the end of my story.

I stare at the flames and listen to the snap and hiss of the fire. I blink and look to the old man, who is as lost in thoughtful fascination as I had been. "Thank you," I say. "Thank you for the gift of your story."

The image of the nest in Raven Keeper's lodge forms in my mind.

I imagine Raven Keeper as she lowers a plump baby into its well of comfort.

I imagine the look of horror on her face as she awakens to a vacant nest.

Wrapped in the pain of Raven Keeper's loss, I sleep.

And dream ...

I shake loose my hair, close my eyes, and lean into the wind. Lift me up, Wind! Release me to the six directions! But my arms remain flesh, and my toes curl into the earth, and for the first time in many moons, the black feathered wings of my dream-world elude me.

I wake before the dawn to the gentle snoring of my host and tuck dried meat and maple sugar beneath his beaver-skin blanket. Moving quietly away, I bow to the incline of the path, a black strand in the darkened underbrush, and push my moccasins against the earth. Muscles loosen as I ease into the rhythm of the climb.

Shadows shift with the dawn. A familiar echo that breathes through the sparse woodland causes my throat to tighten and my heart to pound.

"Craw-cree-craw-cree-craw-craw."

I run to an outcropping of rock and climb to the highest one. My body responds to the sprawling view with a quivering desire to take wing. The familiar sound of the raven call combines with this yearning for flight and I tremble.

"Craw-cree-craw-cree-craw-craw!"

Grandfather Sun casts his rays on Raven Keeper's hill.

The movement in the clearing—could it be?

Raven Keeper's song weaves a mesh around my heart.

"Craw-cree-craw-cree-craw-craw!"

Hand over hand, she draws me into her net. Every measure of my body aches to be by her side and I lower my head to keep from leaping into the treetops below.

Will the ravens—my ravens—hear her call? Will they come for her when they would not come for me? In my panicked departure, I had not thought of that. I look up, but the sky remains bleak and silent. Even the jays and chickadees are still.

Forgive me, Raven Keeper. Your sons are still lost. And I am to blame.

I slide from the rocks and continue my journey in the gray light of the morning. Teardrops splash dark circles on my moccasins, but with every step my determination grows. I learned the raven call, just as Raven Keeper did. I called the ravens, day after day. That was not Old Mother's magic. That was my own achievement, hard-won. And I will win again. I will find a way to save the village from the anger of Man Who Is Raven. Perhaps—dare I wish it?—I will find a way to reunite Raven Keeper with her children.

Raven Keeper has reclaimed her hill. At this, I rejoice. But what of my mother? Gray Wolf will be angry and might harm her. My concern surprises me. Would I mourn a mother who thought of me only as a way to further her own twisted ambitions?

I pull the bone knife from my pouch and consider the curved white blade, yellowed with use. Why couldn't I be more to her? Anger swells in my limbs and I swing the blade against the straight, low branch of a hickory tree. The wood responds with a crackle and hiss. Startled, I lift the knife away. A black scar mars the bark. I press knife to wood once more. The knife sizzles through the thickness of the branch, the limb falls away and the blackened stump emits a string of gray smoke. More of Old Mother's magic. My magic, now.

I trim the branch with easy strokes and fashion a walking stick.

The hickory branch pounds the dry earth and I set my feet against the stony slope. Up I climb, until halted by a wall of rock. I make my way along its base, sure at every turn I will find a way around it. I circle this precipice until Grandfather Sun, trapped behind heavy clouds, begins his descent. There is no way around, no other path to the white peak of Spirit Mountain.

How easy it would be with the wings of a raven!

I pound my fist against the unforgiving wall. "There must be a way," I shout. "I will not give up." I lean my forehead against the cool stone and whisper, "I will not give up."

A puff of gentle mist, with the smell of wet stone, caresses my face. It is gone in less than a moment, but I step back, alert. Above my head is a dark slit I had not seen before.

Grandfather Sun breaks the clouds. I throw the walking stick to the ground and reach for a chink in the stone. My foot finds a gap and I lift my body from the ground. Sweat drips down my back and my fingers turn white with the effort, but I continue, one handhold, one foothold, at a time, to a tiny shelf beside the dark opening.

I remove my pack and slip between the narrow walls. The scent of water blends with the echo of its movement and I sidestep into the mountain. Farther and farther I creep. A black syrup of darkness encases me and my breath rebounds, hot and close. I keep the fingers of one hand outstretched on the rough stone ahead, while the other holds tight to my pack. I fear a sudden drop, or a narrowing that will trap me forever.

A sliver of light appears, as welcome as a torch on a moonless night and I will my body toward it. My breath deepens as the walls widen and I emerge onto a high ledge. An arm's length away, water plummets, white and churning, from high above. With each crash and boom, the waterfall shouts an angry song. Mist tickles my eyelashes and makes me blink. I press a hand against wet rock and peer over the ledge. A winding river flows far below.

Skyward, a soft, sunlit haze floats above the falling current. My perch is among the gray folds of a rocky skirt draped beside the falling water. I know my direction and haul my body from one rock to the other, up and up, until there are no more rocks to climb.

My chest heaves. I lick salty lips and brush rivers of sweat from my eyes. When I can see, the sight renews me. A string of evergreens guards the shores of a quiet lake. The treetops sway and the blue water sparkles with white light. Through the trees, the snowy peak of Spirit Mountain looms large and proud, but here at the water's edge, the air is warm and still.

I can feel neither the pack upon my back nor my feet upon the ground as I walk through the woods along this shore. The air is sweet with pine and birds twitter in the trees. The roar of the waterfall grows distant. On the lake, a pair of black-headed loons splash into long, underwater dives. Gentle waves lap against a fallen tree on a sandy portion of the shoreline.

I sprinkle tobacco from my pouch onto the clear water and give thanks to Great Spirit, our Creator. Then I drop my pack, undress, and slip into the crystal blue.

The water is so cold, it steals my breath. My gasp gives way to a choked laugh and the stinging cold melts into a hazy numbness. I loosen my hair and swim like an otter. I feel clean and new and, for the first time in my waking life, free.

I drip and shiver on the shore as I untie the fur-covered bundle. Rolled tight is Raven Keeper's white skirt and matching tunic. It is what I will wear for the final leg of my journey.

Although I slip often on the ice and snow, the climb to the top is not as difficult as I had imagined. I conquer the incline by propping my feet against jutting rocks and stunted trees. Grandmother Moon lights my way and by the time I reach the peak, the circle of her face crowns the boundless dome of glittering stars. Soon she will begin her descent and Grandfather Sun will rise before she sinks behind the mountain.

Bitter cold blows hard across the peak of Spirit Mountain and shadows of the rocky landscape seem to dance across the moonlit snow. I huddle beside a tall black rock—a poor shield from the wind and the emptiness. How can my ravens live in such a desolate place?

A shadow moves. I turn my head and icy pellets of windswept snow bite my face.

A low growl melts into the whistle of the wind. Is it the rumble of a raven throat? Is it human? I do not know.

One strike of Old Mother's bone knife upon a pile of tinder I have brought with me brings it to fiery life. The flames hop and dance, slaves to the wind. I follow the whirling path of a flying ember, but my eyes stop on a flash of white beyond.

The handle of the knife becomes slippery with the sweat of my palm.

The tiny light flashes double—two parallel pricks of light. I know that sight. It is Grandmother Moon, reflected in yellow eyes.

A mountain lion.

Haunches raised. Head lowered. Ears rigid. The cat is ready to strike. It stares at me across the fire.

"Not now. Not now," I whisper. Without taking my eyes from the hungry beast, I rise and find my voice. "Go away," I shout to the lion. "I must call the ravens."

The great cat leaps before I have finished my command. Its face flies closer, mouth wide. For an instant, I marvel at the white of its fangs and the pink of its tongue. I duck right and its teeth clamp onto my left shoulder. I hear the pop of skin and crunch of bone. Hot arrows of pain erupt in my body.

Barely knowing where to aim the knife, I sink the blade and feel the pressure as it sizzles through the hide. The lion recoils, bounding back from the shock of its injury with a high-pitched scream that dies into an angry growl.

I am on the ground, although I do not remember falling. I clench my fingers, but the knife is no longer in their grasp.

The mountain lion bounces on its back and flips to its feet. Its tongue snaps and its whiskers twitch and it pads toward me, panting. The wound I inflicted is a dark patch on its breast.

My left side anchors me to the ground. I fumble inside my pouch for something, anything, but all I retrieve is the beaded leather band. I shake the strip in the lion's face. "Go away!" I scream. "I cannot die until after the dawn."

Raw anger gleams in the lion's eyes. It lays a heavy paw on my ankle and another on my thigh. It bares its teeth and roars a cat-like cry of victory.

A voice calls from behind the beast. "There is not much meat on that one, my friend."

The great cat snarls and whips its head around. My view is blocked, and pain narrows my vision through this predawn darkness, but my mind absorbs the image of a man, clutching the tail of my attacker.

The lion pounces and the man swings his axe. The axe lands with a thump. The lion falls and rolls across the snow, but rebounds for another attack. The daring hunter stumbles backward, off balance from the blow he dealt.

"Watch out!" I cry. I hurl the beaded band at the cat. How can I think that will distract it?

The animal jumps, and in midflight, the leather strap strikes its fur. But the band does not fall to the ground. It wraps itself tight around the hind leg of the lion.

The lion jerks to the ground, as if yanked by the pull of a rope. As it drops, it stretches its claws and leaves three bloody tracks across the chest of the axe-wielding man. The man does not pause, but runs to the grounded animal and delivers the final blow of death.

He kneels beside the motionless lion. "Forgive me for taking your life, Cousin. May your spirit walk the earth again."

The hunter squats beside me, and through my pain, I sense the smoothness of his face and the soft sleekness of his body. He has not spent many winters as a man. The wind whips his black hair. He smiles at me and the sparkle in his dark eyes is unmistakable.

"Little Trickster!"

He looks at my shoulder and says, "That lion was no match for us, Sister Raven." But there is trace of sorrow and uncertainty in his voice.

Pain radiates to my head. "What is it?"

"Your wound," whispers the lion killer.

Yes, my wound. Perhaps the lion—perhaps he has won, after all.

Images swim before my eyes—memories. Raven Keeper at dawn. Little Foot, like a turtle, poking her head out of her lodge. Old Mother healing the boy. Healing the boy. She pressed herbs to his sores. With the flat of the knife. I do not have herbs. Or know where to find them. But ... but ... perhaps it was not ... not the herbs. No ... not the herbs that healed him.

Weakness overtakes me and each breath is an effort. "Get ... me ... my ... knife."

Little Trickster retrieves my bone knife and eases the handle into the shaking fingers of my right hand. With his guidance, I lift the knife to my torn and bloody shoulder and press the blade against it. In a moment the pain has receded enough for me to see clearly. In more moments, the sting is reduced to an ache, and my heart pumps strength to my bones.

Little Trickster helps me to my feet and I store the knife in my pouch. A smile spreads across his handsome face. His skin glows in the moonlight. I reach up to touch his brown cheek, but he steps back in boyish embarrassment.

"Wait," I say. "You are hurt."

The three tracks on Little Trickster's chest ooze blood. He touches them gingerly and smiles. "This I will show to my brothers, to prove I am fearless."

"Yes, your brothers," I say. The wind has died and the first rays of dawn brush pink across the eastern sky.

Little Trickster follows my gaze as a shadow of worry falls across his face.

I limp to my bundle, drag it out, and loosen the straps as quickly as I can—the fingers of my left hand still do not work properly. I spread my offerings across the snow and shake loose the coat of rabbit skins. I hold it out to Little Trickster. "Look what I have brought."

But he is gone.

"Little Trickster!" My voice chokes. "Little Trickster!"

I turn around and around, searching every shadow. I want him back. As raven and as man, he is a friend. I want him back. My throat tightens into a croak of despair and I sing the raven call from the pit of my belly, from the recesses of my soul.

"Craw-cree-craw-cree-craw-craw!"

Again and again I wail my plea. I want my ravens, my only friends. Not for the village, but for me. Forgive me, Raven Keeper. Forgive me, Gray Wolf. It is not Man Who Is Raven I wish to appease, but my own spirit. It was a selfish quest. I know it now.

I shout to the dawn, "Man Who Is Raven! I have climbed this mountain. I have brought you these offerings. Release your sons. Release them for their mother. Release them for the village. Release them for me!"

The stars fade and Man Who Is Raven answers with ear-shattering silence.

I collapse to my knees. "Then take me. My final offering. I beg you. Do not punish Raven Keeper any longer. Do not threaten the village. Take my life as final payment. I am ready."

I hang my head and wait.

Perhaps I spoke only to the wind. It does not matter. I have lost.

Then I hear it. An echo in the morning breeze. My call coming back to me, to taunt me. But no, it is not my voice. It is a faraway voice. The voice from the hill. Raven Keeper calls.

I lift my head, but the glimmering blue-black of the ravens do not breach the misty pink of the sky.

Raven Keeper sings again, but I am too weary to heed her call. The pain in my shoulder pulses with each beat of my heart. I curl into the soft fur of the coat and close my eyes.

I wake to the afternoon glare of Grandfather Sun. Even in his warmth, I shiver. I move my arm and swallow a groan of pain. My beautiful white tunic, glued to my shoulder with clumps of dried blood, pulls at my wound when I move. I rise and brush my braid behind me. A gentle breeze strokes my face.

Who was I to think I had the power to protect the village? I could have chosen death that night I ran away, when Old Mother hobbled me with the magic of the beaded anklet. I could have run to Raven Keeper and told her to let Gray Wolf kill the witch who is my mother, even if it meant the end of my life. But I was a coward and so all the people of the village will suffer the vengeance of Man Who Is Raven.

A plague of birds and animals will devastate the crop that only now breaks the earth. The men will hunt and fish in the summer and fall, but a lean and hungry winter will follow. The old and the young will perish first. Has Little Foot gone yet to her birthing hut? Will her infant survive?

My eyes fall on the lifeless body of the mountain lion. Sprawled across the snow in the sunlight, it is sad and beautiful. I approach the beast with caution and stroke its yellow fur. The beaded band still circles its paw. I press my knife against the leather and the knot slips free.

I examine the small white beads on the band and the white curve of the knife. Magic for the hunt. Magic for fire and for healing. My fingers tighten around the handle of the knife. By the lake of the loons, hidden and peaceful, I could survive on my own. The worst would be the loneliness—although I am used to that.

But no. This magic will be needed in the village, to ease the suffering that is sure to come. I gather my pack, follow my own tracks down the snowy peak and seek the comfort of the

Hidden Lake.

When I dip my hand in the water, tiny ripples disturb the perfect reflection of blue sky and white clouds. I pause only long enough to clean my wound and change my bloodied tunic.

Beside the roar of the waterfall, I lower myself from rock to rock. I dangle a leg and probe for the next foothold. I slip—gather a short breath—my foot finds solid ground. This instant of fright is repeated as I descend, and the rush of air beside the swift cascade adds to my feeling of unbalance.

Although my shoulder still aches each time I lift my arm or grasp a ledge or lean upon my elbow, I continue to descend, hoping at every gap and shadow that I have found the passageway to the mountain's face.

Is the river closer than it appeared when I emerged to the waterfall the day before? Have I descended too far? I climb, this time closer to the spray of water, where the rocks are wet and dripping. My fingers are raw and my frustration wells with the pain in my shoulder. Like an ant scuttling aimlessly along the curves of a bark lodge, I am lost among the crags and rocks.

My throat emits a tight grunt as I hike my body up to a sharp-edged stone. But a foreign noise was mixed with mine and I listen. The faint sound of an animal, high pitched. Again I hear it. It is a dog barking, far in the distance. I stand tall and find it slightly louder. I lean left and it is louder still. I follow the sound of this dog, higher up and closer to the falls.

There it is—the ledge and opening, hidden by a curved brown stone. I hoist myself up, clutch the bundle with my good hand, and sidestep into the mountain passage.

A cool breeze blows across the outer slope of the mountainside. The vibrating loudness of the waterfall is a dull drone and my ears ring with the persistent yaps of a small black dog on the ground below me. A man squats beside the dog, examining the walking stick I had discarded at the base of the wall. I see his bare back, leggings, and long, loose hair.

"Little Trickster!" I cry.

Startled, he looks up, falls on his back, and opens his eyes wide at me. It is not Little Trickster, but Two Feathers. He stares at me, open-mouthed, while his dog makes twirling, barking leaps.

Two Feathers scrambles to his feet. He gives a gruff command, as if the dog were the reason he had fallen in fright, and not my exclamation from above.

I toss my bundle down, hang by the ledge—with no small amount of pain in my shoulder—and drop to the ground.

Gray dust adheres to the sweat on my skin and my clothes are stained from two days of hard travel. The speechless state of Two Feathers is, no doubt, due in part to my appearance. He recovers some of his dignity with a lift of his chin, but his eyes flick to the ledge above, and his mouth opens in astonishment.

The rock wall is solid stone, with no visible sign of an opening. Like the heart of Man Who Is Raven, Spirit Mountain is closed.

Two Feathers' bow leans against the rock and his quiver, sewn from the pelt of a fox, lies across the dry earth. To take his attention away from what he must consider fearful magic, I say the first words that come to me: "Do you hunt?" I wince, but he is too distracted to notice the foolishness of my question.

He turns his eyes to me and takes a moment to focus on my face. "Yes. No. Gray Wolf, my father, sent me to bring you back."

"He sent you—alone?"

Two Feathers' eyes narrow, as if my question had been dipped in scorn. "We lost your trail, and so the others returned."

"And you?"

"I would not abandon the search."

My heart leaps when I imagine that Two Feathers might have been driven by some attachment to me, but I quickly turn my back on these thoughts. He is more likely anxious to present me as a prize to his father.

Two Feathers picks up his bow and quiver. "Will you go freely to the village?"

"I will."

He considers me for some time. "At dawn, you called the ravens. I heard your voice on the mountaintop."

I hang my head. It is hard to talk of my failure. "The ravens did not come. Man Who Is Raven is not appeased."

Two Feathers straightens his back. "We will go to Gray Wolf," he says, and walks away with the black dog at his heels.

I fling my pack across my healthy shoulder and follow.

Our moccasins make a soft, uneven cadence as they part the blades of grass that sway and whisper in the evening breeze. Only the black points of the dog's ears show as it makes a fluttering path through waves of sallow green. The sloping meadow is unfamiliar to me, but I am content to follow the easy swing of the foxtail that hangs from the quiver at Two Feathers' back.

Few flowers bloom on the cusp of spring and so I pause at a cluster of blossoms the color of sunset. A year ago, Old Mother told Raven Keeper she dreamt of the missing child, crying near flowers such as these. A shiver vibrates across my tired shoulders. Seven flowers bloom, like Raven Keeper's seven children. I touch the soft, red-orange of each one. Always First. Proud Beak. Observes From Trees. Restless Lookout. Flies Too Far. Little Trickster. I pluck the seventh and look around me.

There is no one in the meadow but Two Feathers, who watches me as if I were some mysterious creature of the forest. My eyes linger on the two feathers that hang from his hair. He is close to the age of Little Trickster. Could it be?

The dog barks in the distance, then yelps and whimpers. Two Feathers turns to the sound, then runs toward the woods at the base of the meadow. My pack bounces on my back as I follow.

We find the black dog thrashing at the base of a tree. White foam and blood ooze from its mouth. Partway up the white birch is a frightened porcupine. Its quills are raised and its barbed tail whips back and forth.

Two Feathers extends his arms to the dog, but the animal convulses in pain and fright. Two Feathers lays down his bow and unsheathes the knife at his waist. His eyes shine in the last lingering light of the day and he takes a sorrowful breath. "I am sorry, my friend. I will ease your suffering."

"No!" I cry.

Two Feathers' love for the animal trembles through his words. "The quills are in his mouth. If I do not end his life now, he will starve to death and die in pain."

He raises his knife and advances, but I grab his arm. "Please," I say, "give me a chance."

My touch releases some of the taut urgency that ripples through his body. Two Feathers stares at me and finally relents.

I find the bloodied tunic in my pack and instruct Two Feathers to wrap the body of his dog tight within it. When this is done, I lift Old Mother's bone knife to the dog's writhing mouth.

What am I doing? I was fortunate to heal the bones of my shoulder. But this is an instrument of magic and I hardly know its ways. The gamble is not only with the life of the dog but also with the trust of the man. If one is lost, then so are both.

I press the flat of the knife against the snout of the wild-eyed animal. One by one, the barbed quills, embedded in snout and cheeks and tongue, fall away.

Two Feathers carries his pet, wrapped tight within my tunic, to a stream that lies in a thickness of trees farther down the mountain, and washes its muzzle. He scolds the dog with a voice that falters. "You are ... a foolish beast ... and a poor hunter."

The impatient dog wriggles free, leaps to the shore, and shakes the water from its coat. On its scrawny body, the black fur sticks out in slick points. It perks its ears and tilts its head, as if confused by our attention, and Two Feathers and I laugh together.

The dog bounds into the forest.

Two Feathers lowers his voice. "Thank you for the life of my dog."

I look at the ground in an effort to contain the uneasy joy I feel. I have won the gamble, and perhaps his trust, but a question nags me. "We should move on," I say. "Perhaps ... perhaps your wife waits for you."

"Wife?" Two Feathers' bow drops from his hands. He turns his face away as he retrieves it. "I do not have a wife." Two Feathers, the brave hunter, stumbles once, then takes long strides into the woodland.

Somehow, my pack seems lighter. I swing it across my back and follow Two Feathers and his leaping dog through the trees. Little Foot, it seems, does not have the husband I thought she had.

Night comes quickly to the woodland. Two Feathers' pace does not falter, and I am tempted to suggest that we rest, when I come upon my guide, crouched in the brush. I smell the tobacco as I stoop beside him. Through the branches, I see an old man sitting by a fire. Smoke from his pipe floats before his face and when he draws on the stem, the embers cast an eerie light on his wrinkled skin.

I whisper to Two Feathers, "I know this person. I sat with him my first night on the mountain."

Two Feathers does not take his eyes from the old man. "We followed your trail," he murmurs. "There were no signs of another."

"You were mistaken." I walk ahead to greet the storyteller before Two Feathers can answer.

"It is Sister Raven, Grandfather, and I bring Two Feathers. May we share your fire?" I loosen my bundle and extract a quantity of dried meat and walnuts. I retie the offerings and place them behind the old man. I had wished to give the coat and all its contents to Man Who Is Raven. But these few things would be well used by the old man and making this gift somehow lessens the sting of my failure.

The old man thanks me with a slight nod of his head.

Two Feathers lingers in the brush, but joins us when I sit to distribute the food. He remains rigid when he squats and does not set down his fox-quiver and bow. The dog bends its tail low and growls at the old man. Two Feathers throws a portion of meat outside our circle of light and the dog quiets.

When we are finished with the meal, the old man says, "I wish to tell a story."

Two Feathers comes down from his heels and rests his bow and quiver. In the firelight, I watch the muscles in his face soften. I allow myself, then, to become lost in the words of the storyteller.

Of times not long past.

There was a young husband and wife who lived in the village of the Twin Lakes. One winter night, while the husband was away, a stranger came to their lodge. "I have traveled far," he said. "My body is cold and craves meat." The wife let the man sit by her fire, but offered him only corn gruel. "Is that not the fresh cooked meat of a beaver I smell?" said the man. "I have no meat to share," said the wife. "Is that not the fresh skin of a beaver I see?" said the man. "I have no meat to share," said the wife. The man stood. He hobbled to the shadows of the lodge and lifted a woven mat to reveal a clay pot. The steam of fresh beaver stew rose to his face. "I am sorry for you," said the man, and he left.

When the wife went to the woods with the women to draw sap from the maple trees, whispers buzzed around her face like mosquitoes. "There is the woman who hides her food." "There is the woman who lies." For all the days of the maple sugaring, she heard this, and she became very angry. She stomped her anger into the snow, one foot after the other, until she was very deep into the forest. There she sat upon a rotting log beside a gnarled oak tree and spoke. "How they ridicule me! How they stare and whisper! I will make them swallow their chatter. I will make them tremble before me!"

The icy leaves at the base of the tree cracked and buckled and the wife jumped up in fright. A snout poked through the frost, followed by the great black head of a sleepy bear. Too frightened to move, the wife watched the bear emerge from its den beneath the roots of the gnarled oak tree. The bear shook its baggy coat, reared up on its hind legs, and became a man. Dressed in a bearskin robe, with a necklace of bear claws around his thick neck, Man Who Is Bear spoke to the wife. "Brave words woke me from my winter sleep. Is the heart as brave as the words?"

The wife's lingering anger gave her strength and she stood tall before Man Who Is Bear.

"Ha," said Man Who Is Bear. "Perhaps you have the right heart. Come into my den and rest."

The wife knew that if she rested in the bear's den, her nose would grow long, hair would grow over her body, and her fingers would become claws. If she slept in the home of Man Who Is Bear, she would become a bear herself. So she said, "Rest I would, if I could think only of myself. But the people of my village suffer and they need me. If you give me what I seek, I would return to the village and say 'Look what Man Who Is Bear has given us! Look what is sent by Bear, the most revered of all the animals!'"

"What is it you want?" said Man Who Is Bear.

"The way of medicines and healing herbs, which is known to your kind."

"Very well," said Man Who Is Bear. "I will give you what you want. But you must use the knowledge only for good and when four seasons have passed, you must tell your husband you will be the wife of another, and return to me."

"Agreed," said the wife.

Man Who Is Bear imparted the knowledge of healing plants to the wife and then burrowed back into the roots of the gnarled oak tree.

The wife returned to the maple grove, where the women were gathered around a little girl who had been burned by boiling sap. The wife approached the girl with an herb salve that soothed the flesh and lessened the pain. From that time forward, the wife was called Herb Woman.

Herb Woman cured small ailments for payment of food and trinkets, but she did not honor Man Who Is Bear as she said she would. And in some cases, in some terrible cases, she twisted the knowledge to do harm. To the first woman who had once spoken of her with sarcasm and disdain, Herb Woman gave boils on all parts of her body. To the second, painful joints.

And so Herb Woman lived for all the moons of the spring and the summer and the fall. Under the Snow Blinder Moon, before the sap flowed again in the maple trees, Herb Woman said to her husband, "In the village I am admired for my skills, but I feel the shadows of suspicion when I heal."

"You are my wife and have respect as a healer," said the husband. "You should not need more than that."

"If you killed a bear," said Herb Woman, "we would be honored at the feast."

"Only once have the spirits deemed me worthy to slay one of that kind," said the young husband. "Once I dreamed of a bear who spoke to me and said, 'That is where you are going to find me,' and I found the bear and killed him, but I have not dreamed so since."

"Ah," said Herb Woman, "you do not need a dream to tell you where to find the bear. I will bring you to it."

And so the husband prepared for the hunt and followed his wife to the gnarled oak tree. He leaned over the breathing hole of the snow-covered den and addressed the bear. "Cousin, it is time to come out. The winter has been long and we are hungry. Allow yourself to be killed!"

A long snout broke the snow and a sleepy head pushed through the white powder. The husband struck the bear with a club, as this was the right way to slay a bear. The bear snorted and growled. The husband struck again and again until finally the animal lay dead.

"Please do not be angry, Cousin," said the husband. "I killed you only because I am poor and hungry. I thank you for your *sacrifice."*

Herb Woman and her husband dragged the carcass back to the village and shared the meat in a great feast, where they were honored. Then, as was the custom, the bones were boiled and given to the hunter, to be returned to the den. But Herb Woman knew that the spirit of Man Who Is Bear would be complete if all his bones lay together again below the gnarled oak, and he would come back to life, and seek her out. When none were looking, she stole a handful of tiny bones and two sharp claws. The tiny bones and the largest claw she hid beneath her sleeping skin and the smaller claw she hid in the pocket of her skirt.

But Man Who Is Raven, in his raven form, circled the sky above, and watched Herb Woman steal the precious bones. He flew to the gnarled oak to wait.

When the husband arrived at the den, there was Man Who Is Raven, in his human form, with shining black hair and eyes set slightly wide, squatting on the lowest branch of the gnarled oak.

"It is a foolish hunter who does not return the bones of his cousin, the Bear," said Man Who Is Raven.

"I honor the Bear and offer him all of his bones," said the husband.

"It is a foolish husband, then," said Man Who Is Raven, "who does not check the pockets of his wife."

Before the husband could reply, Man Who Is Raven grew glossy wings and flew away.

The husband returned to his lodge, thrust his hand into his wife's pocket and found the small claw. "You shame me!" he cried. "Man Who Is Raven saw you and told me you stole the bones. Go out of my sight. You are no longer my wife!"

Herb Woman gathered a pack for travel and once more stomped her anger into the snow, one foot after the other, until she was very far from the village. Only one thought made her smile, and that was her secret knowledge of the tiny bones and the sharp claw wrapped in her sleeping skin.

She sharpened the claw into a dagger and sewed the tiny bones onto a leather band. These two items she found to contain much magic. When she lay the leather band, carefully beaded with the bear's bones, in a circle on the ground, it leapt up and grabbed tight to the leg of any animal that passed. The animal could not run away and the enchantment would not be released until Herb Woman closed her eyes and pressed the claw dagger against the knot. The dagger itself could make fire whenever she had need of it. With this magic, Herb Woman survived her banishment.

For many winters, Herb Woman traveled from village to village, offering her healing arts for profit. But never earning the reverence she craved, she always moved on. Early one morning, she heard a raven call. The hairs on her neck bristled as she thought of Man Who Is Raven, the one she blamed for her exile.

She came upon a hunter setting traps in the forest. "What manner of raven makes that call at dawn?" asked Herb Woman.

"It is not a raven," said the hunter. "It is the wife of Man Who Is Raven. Each morning, from her home high on a hill, she calls to her husband and six of her children. They fly to her as ravens and then transform into man and boys. At dusk, husband and sons fly away again to the peak of Spirit Mountain. In the night, the wife sleeps alone with her seventh child, an infant not yet ready to take flight."

Herb Woman designed a plan of revenge. As the wife of Man Who Is Raven slept, Herb Woman crept into the lodge, scooped up their child from the circular bed of sticks and earth, and hurried from the hill. The infant squirmed and blinked. Herb Woman unsheathed her bone dagger. She meant to end the budding life then, but thought quickly of another plan and tied the leather band of bones around the tiny ankle.

She carried the child, thus tethered, in a cradleboard on her back, across hills and valleys, for more than the cycle of a moon, and returned to the lodge of her husband.

"See what I have here?" she said. "A child of the spirits. You must take us in and honor us."

The lonely hunter had not taken another wife and lived each day mourning the loss of the family he never had. He did not fear his wife, shrunken and bent from years of wandering, but pitied her and took her in. The child, he loved as his own. The husband never guessed that the beads on the little one's anklet were the bones of the bear he had killed many winters past. He never guessed that the child he loved was bonded to his wife by magic, or that the little girl-child was the daughter of Man Who Is Raven.

"Wait!" I cry. "It is not a daughter. Raven Keeper's seventh child is a son, like the rest."

The old man raises his head and his milky eyes reflect the fire. "Perhaps you do not wish to know this story."

My thoughts scatter like leaves in the wind. Herb Woman is so much like Old Mother. And what can this mean, that Raven Keeper had a daughter? Old Mother told me Raven Keeper left her hill in search of a son. But, oh, how easily lies roll from Old Mother's tongue!

And what of this beaded band? My ankle still bears the mark of the one I wore all my life—the broken band I carry in my rabbit-skin pouch. The old man, my host, has the answers and will reveal them in his own time. I take a deep breath and swallow hard. "Forgive me, Grandfather. I wish to know your story."

The old man lowers his eyelids, ready to return to the trance of the story. I rouse every bit of my will to silence the questions in my mind and concentrate on his words.

For a time, Herb Woman enjoyed the respect she earned as mother, but more and more she was bothered by the loving attention paid to the toddler by her husband. One night, in the third winter of her return, Herb Woman gathered a pack for travel and stole away with the child. She traveled across hills and valleys, for more than the cycle of a moon and came again to the river village, in order to learn the fate of the wife of Man Who Is Raven, and see if there was a profit to be made with the girl. Again, Herb Woman heard the raven call at dawn.

She came upon a woman, gathering firewood in the forest. "What manner of raven makes that call at dawn?" asked Herb Woman.

"It is not a raven," said the woman. "It is the wife of Man Who Is Raven. Each morning, from her home high on a hill, she calls to her six children. They fly to her as ravens and remain as ravens for all of the daylight. At dusk, they fly away to their father, who lives at the peak of Spirit Mountain. She never sees her children in their human form. It is a punishment her husband inflicted—he blames her for the loss of their seventh child, three winters ago. The people of the village fear Man Who Is Raven and revere his wife. They bring her offerings at each full moon and these she sends with her raven children at every dusk, when they fly back to Spirit Mountain."

So, *thought Herb Woman.* Raven Keeper receives prayers and offerings while I raise her brat. Well, we will see what can be done.

Herb Woman built a small hut in the village. She presented the child as her own and offered herself as healer. Soon enough, Herb Woman set the child to spy on Raven Keeper so the girl could learn her ways. When the girl became a young woman, Herb Woman sent Raven Keeper away by trickery. The girl, not knowing her true birth, and tethered by Herb Woman's magical anklet, called the ravens in Raven Keeper's place.

I jump to my feet. "But that is me, Grandfather. I am Sister Raven. It is my story you tell."

The old man closes his eyes and sets his mouth.

"My apologies, Grandfather. Please forgive me." I sit again and grip my elbows in order to quell the wild shudder through my arms.

The old man lowers his head and is silent.

I collect my thoughts and steady my breathing, but can hardly suppress my emotions. The question flies from my lips before I can stop it. "Grandfather, did Raven Keeper know it was—I was—her ... her daughter?"

The old man lifts his head and a tiny wisp of a black feather drifts from the cascade of white hair on his shoulders. "Of course the mother knew. She knew the voice of her only daughter the first morning she heard the girl call her brothers. But she feared Herb Woman's deadly power over the girl and kept her silence."

My throat tightens. Mother. Brothers. It is almost too much at once. But there is more I must know. "What of Man Who Is Raven? He sent the ravens—his six sons—he sent them to me. Did he think that Raven Keeper called? Was he deceived?"

The old man's eyebrows come together. "Deceived? Man Who Is Raven was not deceived." He sits up straight and tall and the milky haze of his old eyes clears.

I feel Two Feathers' body stiffen beside me.

The cobweb of lines in the old man's face thin and disappear, and his white hair darkens to black. He shrugs the beaver robe from brown shoulders and glides to his feet. A striking warrior stands before me, with piercing eyes set slightly wide. His shining black hair flows to his knees and there are many black feathers woven into it. From the stories I have been told these past nights, I recognize him at once.

Two Feathers jumps up and unsheathes his flint knife.

With trembling limbs, I come to my feet before Man Who Is Raven.

Man Who Is Raven shows Two Feathers the palm of his hand and speaks to me. "I was not deceived. When you sang to the mountain in your mother's place, I knew that voice could only belong to my daughter. Hah, I suspected the truth of your birth when I saw that old witch drag a girl of three winters into the village. Could it be, I wondered, that it was Herb Woman who stole my daughter from the lodge? I watched you as you grew from girl to woman, looked for signs of your heritage, but you were timid and weak, and I thought, 'The raven spirit does not reside in that one!'"

My cheeks burn with a jumble of emotions I cannot distinguish. "All this time ... since I called—how could you ... why ... why didn't you ... speak out?"

The shoulders of Man Who Is Raven stiffen with pride. "I wished to know your spirit."

Know my spirit? Is my life a game to be played by someone else? Anger overwhelms me and I forget to be afraid. "And now? Why ... why did you pretend to be an old man and tell me these tales?"

"It is time you knew the truth of your birth."

Hah! Truth! The journey of my life has been made across a swamp made treacherous with untruths. Never did I walk on the solid ground of love and acceptance. No, every step I took was with the risk of unknown depths and dangers. "You are so full of tricks," I cry. "How can I know if your words are true?"

The eyes of Man Who Is Raven narrow. "Do you dare to doubt me?"

Doubt him? Hot pain pounds against my temples. I take short, shallow breaths as I consider all he has told me. My dreams. My raven voice. The tether. Like stepping stones in the bog, the pieces of his stories feel sure beneath my feet. No, I do not doubt him. I know who I am. I know it now. But the fire of anger still burns in my heart and my words hiss like flames. "You kept me from my mother."

My father's lips form a surly smile. "How many times did you spy on Raven Keeper? My sons saw you hidden there. Did I ever stop you from going to her? Did I?"

The unfairness of his words chokes my breath. "But ... but you knew my fate and never spoke."

"As long as you bowed to the witch, I did not wish to claim you." Man Who Is Raven lifts his chin and looks down his long, straight nose. "When you escaped her magic, hunh, that is when I saw myself in you. That is when I considered you Daughter."

"Do not! Do not call me Daughter. You deprived me of my true mother and deprived my mother of the flesh and blood of her sons. You blamed her when I was taken. Then you blamed the village. Well, you should have blamed yourself. Every night, you left her alone. Her child, me—I was ... was kidnapped by someone, someone who sought vengeance on you—not her! Raven Keeper has suffered terrible pain and loneliness. Do you understand the wounds you have inflicted? Do you ever think of it?"

I take a faltering breath. "The village reveres you. With every moon, Gray Wolf thanks you. You talk of truth. Now I know the truth of you. You are a cruel and heartless being. I am ashamed to be your daughter."

I regret my last words as soon as they are spoken. If I could retrieve them from the air and swallow them back, I would. Who am I to judge this man? And I am not ashamed. But I am proud of who I am, more proud than I have ever been.

My father's hair lifts from his shoulders, as if blasted by a strong wind. Black plumes fly from the billowing hair of Man Who Is Raven and settle on his skin. His arms blacken with layers of feathers and become wings. His nose and chin lengthen into a beak and his legs narrow and curve into the sharp claws of a raven.

Two Feathers and I step back. The dog plants its front paws wide and growls.

The mighty black bird thrusts his wings wide with a rush of air that blows cool upon my face. He raises and lowers the black-feathered wings at his sides and sails into the air. His wingtip brushes my cheek as he makes a tight arc back to the ground to snatch up my fur-covered pack—the bundle of offerings I had carried to the mountain for Man Who Is Raven, and had gifted to him, unknowingly, when he had taken the form of an old man. The feathers whoosh and rustle. The air shivers with his guttural cry. "Crok! Crok!"

And Man Who Is Raven flies into the darkness.

I press both hands to my burning cheeks. "What have I done?" I murmur. "What have I done?"

Two Feathers reaches up, as if to touch my shoulder, but withdraws his hand. "You ... you spoke with courage."

"No, no." I say. "It is not brave to speak in anger."

Two Feathers' shoulders relax and he slips his knife into the sheath at his belt. "Tonight we should rest, and tomorrow, return to the village. Gray Wolf will know what to do."

A flood of tears stream down my cheeks and drip from my chin. The gentleness of Two Feathers does little to relieve the grief of my failure.

Two Feathers and I start early and travel fast, both anxious to distance ourselves from the night's confrontation. We reach Raven Keeper's hill by midday. I am light and quick without my pack and when we break from the woodland, I scamper up the slope with feet and hands, and send loose stones tumbling behind me.

She is there, in the clearing. Raven Keeper. My mother.

I fall to my knees at her feet. My chest heaves. My breath is short. I cannot speak. I cannot see. I can only feel her hands on me, raising me to my feet. Then her arms around me.

"My little one," she whispers. "My own."

I bury my face in the sweetness of her hair and lift my arms to complete the embrace. It is a new experience and it is a memory, all at once. I am the infant, lost in the warm circle of a mother's love. I am the woman, come home.

I do not know how long we stay this way before we slip apart. Tears stain my mother's cheeks. The dust of my journey adheres to her dress.

She takes my hand and leads me into the lodge. She washes my face and hands, feeds me bowls full of fish stew and brings me water in a shining turtle shell. We do not speak until I cannot eat another bite.

"I saw Little Trickster," I say. "He helped me on the mountain."

A haze of sadness drifts across my mother's eyes.

Perhaps I should not have mentioned my brother—a knot of regret tightens my belly. "He is strong and well," I say.

Raven Keeper's smile is tinged with sorrow.

I yearn to hear her voice again. "Where is Two Feathers?"

"Gone to Gray Wolf, to speak of your return, my daughter."

My daughter. The melody my mother sings is the sweetest I have ever known. I can hardly bear to enjoy the full truth of it. But fear bloodies my joy and I shudder. "Gray Wolf warned me not to leave the hill."

Raven Keeper touches my hand. "I have known Gray Wolf since we were children. He is known to be harsh, but he is never unfair."

"And what of Old Mother?" I ask. "What became of her?"

"She lives in her old hut in the village. I take a bowl of gruel to her every day." There is a flash of the same sparkle I have seen in Little Trickster's eyes. "But I cannot be sure she trusts me enough to eat it."

Too soon for me, Gray Wolf arrives with Two Feathers. This is the first time in many moons that I have seen Gray Wolf without the red paint and wolf mantle of the offering ceremony. We sit on mats around the fire pit outside the lodge while Two Feathers' dog lounges in the shade.

Has it been just three days? It seems a lifetime ago. I speak of all that happened since I woke too late to call the ravens. My hands tremble and my voice shakes as I begin, but soon my body relaxes into the rhythm of my story and I am no longer afraid. Gray Wolf's dark eyes are open to my tale, and where I expected sternness and punishment, there is understanding and respect. I tell them of the Hidden Lake and the mountain lion. I tell them of Little Trickster and the beaded anklet.

Two Feathers sits stiff with importance, but sometimes I watch his eyes grow wide with childlike wonder. The eyes of Raven Keeper do not rise from the fire stones.

When I am finished, Two Feathers tells his own story, from the time he left with the group of men who tracked me to the mountain, to our encounter with Man Who Is Raven. "Sister Raven blames herself," says Two Feathers. "But she showed much courage as she faced him."

My face burns with embarrassment and I catch the hint of a smile on my mother's lips.

"You have acted well," says Gray Wolf. "Both of you. There is little more that can be done."

"I will call the ravens at the dawn," says Raven Keeper.

"Sister Raven may join me—if she wishes, and then—then we shall see."

Gray Wolf nods his head in agreement, then pulls out the sandstone pipe that is tucked in his waistband. Raven Keeper adds a short branch to the fire.

They act as if it is settled. But it is not settled. Not for me. "There must be more we can do," I say. "Something more than just wait and see."

Gray Wolf takes a pinch of tobacco from the small pouch that hangs from his neck and presses it into the pipe with his thumb. With a green stick, he fishes through the ashes and rolls a tiny ember into the bowl of his pipe. He brings the stem to his lips and, with faraway eyes, watches the smoke curl toward the sky.

"One day," says the sachem, "two brothers put their canoes into the waters of a river unknown to them. They were in search of an island said to be rich in game, an island that could be reached only by an upriver journey of four days. The river current was strong, but these two men were also strong. For three days and three nights they traveled, and each day, the force of the river grew.

"On the fourth day, when their strength was almost gone, they saw the island ahead in the distance. The first brother said, 'The river is too mighty and we cannot win.' The second brother said, 'No, we must never give in to the river.'

"The first brother put down his paddle and let the current carry him. When he came to a tree limb that jutted from the shore, his arms were rested. He grabbed hold of the limb, pulled himself from the canoe, and saved his own life.

"The second brother continued to push his canoe through the white-capped water. When he was a spear's throw from the island, the last of his strength left him and he collapsed. The mighty river overturned the second brother's canoe and his life was lost."

Gray Wolf draws deep on his pipe and offers the smoke to the heavens. "Sometimes it is foolish to fight the current. Sometimes it is better to let it carry you."

I sigh. "And like the river, my father cannot be conquered."

Gray Wolf's smile travels from his lips to his eyes and he points the stem of his pipe at my heart. "Perhaps you have the wisdom of the first brother."

The shadows are long and Gray Wolf and Two Feathers disappear onto the path into the village. Raven Keeper leads me into our lodge and presses her lips to my forehead. I am dizzy with pleasure of her kiss and weary beyond words. I lie on my familiar space in the lodge, on the bench cushioned with corn husks and deerskin, and fall into a dreamless sleep.

It is time.

I hold my mother's hand in the clearing as Grandfather Sun's first orange rays breathe Spirit Mountain to life. Hours before sunrise, we had bathed in the spring, washed and braided each other's hair, and dressed for the dawn.

Now we sing. We sing to the mountain. We sing to the ravens. We sing to the family we crave.

"Craw-cree-craw-cree-craw-craw!"

There is pleading in my mother's voice.

"Craw-cree-craw-cree-craw-craw!"

There is apology and remorse in mine.

Six dots speckle the snowy mountaintop, so far away I wonder if I only imagine them. Six black spots fall around each other like leaves in the wind—larger and larger, closer and closer.

Raven Keeper releases my hand and lifts both arms into the air. Her mouth opens in maternal desire. I step away and let her greet her sons.

The ravens talk to each other, chattering all at once. "Craw!" "Cree!" "Craw!" They dance and swoop to the hill, to the clearing where Raven Keeper waits. They circle around her. They call to her, greet her. Their wings brush her hands. Then six ravens scatter to the trees.

Raven Keeper wipes silent tears from her cheeks.

Bittersweet is this reunion, for these are ravens, and not

men—feathered, and not flesh. I am about to shout to Man Who Is Raven, to beg him to release my mother from her loneliness, but a movement distracts me.

A young man walks from the woods that surround the clearing. He is tall and straight and the fringe on his leggings ripples in perfect waves. Long hair slips from his shoulders as he inclines his head and lets Raven Keeper stroke his face.

Always First! I bite my lip to keep from calling out.

Next, from the woods opposite, struts Proud Beak. He is not as tall as Always First, but broader of chest. All of his head is shaved but for a circle of hair that grows into a long braid down his back. Straight-lined tattoos in delicate, repeating patterns decorate the length of his arms and legs. Proud Beak brings Raven Keeper's hand to his cheek.

Observes From Trees, with a raccoon tail dangling from hair gathered haphazardly at the base of his neck, stays half-hidden behind an elm before venturing to greet his mother. In that time, Restless Lookout walks the perimeter of the clearing with cautious steps. His lone strip of cropped hair makes a fan that bounces as he walks. Raven Keeper reaches out to Observes From Trees and then to Restless Lookout, and draws them both into her circle.

At full speed, and with a great whoop, the fifth son crashes into the clearing from behind the lodge. It can only be Flies Too Far. Of all my brothers, he has a face most like our father's—or how our father's face could appear, if flushed with happiness. Flies Too Far swings his mother around and around. He releases her and Restless Lookout reaches out just in time to prevent Raven Keeper from flying to the ground.

I do not hear Little Trickster emerge from the trees behind me. He brushes my elbow as he walks past, his face intent on the woman surrounded by all her sons but one. I detect the glimmer of a tear in his eye—a tear I know he is loath to expose to his brothers. He catches Raven Keeper up in a quick, intense embrace and releases her into the circle of her children.

Raven Keeper's joy transforms her face. She is a little girl, caught in a quandary of too many pleasures. I think of all the years I had observed her as I was hidden in the bracken that lies behind me now, never knowing she was my mother—never knowing she could ever own this kind of happiness.

Never knowing that I could own it too.

My mother looks to me. Our eyes meet. She reaches her arms, beckoning me. It is the image in my dream, the dream I had the night I ran away from Old Mother. In that dream, a bear held a cord that drew me back—the bear was Old Mother and she pulled my feet from under me. But this is not a dream. My spirit flies, unhindered, at Raven Keeper's welcome, and I go to her.

My mother takes my hands in hers while my brothers surround me. They talk to me all at once. "This is Little Sister." "Sturdy, for a girl." "Too skinny." They pat my back and rub my hair. I cower at their roughness, and laugh.

And laugh.

And laugh.

I do not wish to see her face. Not now. Not at the end of the first day I have spent with my family. But she comes, as beautiful as ever, framed by the deep blue of the sky. Grandmother Moon hovers low, ready to claim the heavens.

I stand with Raven Keeper in the clearing. Our shadows stretch long before us as we face Spirit Mountain. "My mother, is it the gift of a day, or a lifetime?"

Raven Keeper is silent. She does not know the answer any more than I do. Like the brothers of Gray Wolf's story, we ride a current too powerful to battle.

Thin shadows, like fingers, slide between our feet—shadows cast by my brothers as they approach softly and join us in the clearing.

With a nod from Always First, my brothers turn their backs and take solemn steps into the woodland. Trees and shrubs swallow them into the dense forest.

By Raven Keeper's side, I watch the quiet hills soften into evening.

"Crawk!" A raven breaks from the trees and crosses the sky. Always First fans black wings and circles the clearing.

Raven Keeper takes my hand in hers.

From the trees, two more ravens take flight. Proud Beak and Observes From Trees.

I grip my mother's hand.

Three more ravens join the others—Restless Lookout, Flies Too Far, and Little Trickster. Six black birds beat life into the sky above the clearing. Their voices split the chill, gray air.

I lift my chin and feel the movement of the air upon my face. Oh, how I wish I could fly among them! How I wish I could fly as I had flown in my dreams! How I wish I could fly and not fly alone!

Raven Keeper is behind me, although I did not feel her let go of my hand. She tugs at my braid and I hear the leather tie drop to the grass. I imagine the grace of her fingers as they unravel the weave, one strand at a time. I think of Old Mother, who used magic to untie the knot of my anklet. There is no magic in Raven Keeper's fingers. Only love.

I shake my head and the wind whips the length of my hair. I close my eyes and delight in the restless tugging at my scalp.

When I lift my arms, it is like a dream. My dream. On my toes, I lean into the wind. Lift me up, Wind! Release me to the six directions!

My feet brush the grasses of the clearing and when I open my eyes ... when I open my eyes—

I slice the air with black wings. Feathers rustle as air speeds across their massive span. Head tucked and claws curled, my body merges with the might of the wind. Freedom. Power. Animal pleasure. These are mine.

I open my beak and drink the twilight breeze.

Always First squawks and trills and I know, as if he had spoken with a human tongue, that he said, "Follow me!"

My brother ravens fly away, their black bodies a silhouette of graceful motion against the gray mass of Spirit Mountain.

I lean into a high arc for one last glimpse of my mother. Her face is colored by joy, but outlined in sorrow.

"Cree. Crok-crok," I shout to her. *I will return!*

I flap my wings to catch up to the shrinking raven silhouettes. Darkness engulfs us as I come upon them. I feel my brothers around me, feel the ripples of air that radiate from the motion of their wings and tails. We fly close but do not collide. We fly fast. Faster than I ever flew in my dreams. Soon we are coasting above the Hidden Lake, high up, near the peak of Spirit Mountain.

I follow my raven brothers to a far shore. Strewn about in the shadows are the remnants of their human life on the mountaintop. Two small lodges. A fire pit. Three-pronged spears laid out beside a scattered pile of blackened torches, and three dugout canoes. I had assumed the ravens lived on the snow-covered peak, but it is here they had spent their human nights—by the lake of the loons.

Little Trickster almost topples me with a flick of his wing under mine.

"Crok-crok-creee!" I screech.

My brothers dive at me, tease me. I swoop and bank with ease. Play. It is new and, at first, strange, but I quickly make a natural seventh in their nocturnal games.

Observes From Trees tires first and flutters into the arms of a tall pine. Restless Lookout makes a lazy spiral into the budding branches of an oak. Flies Too Far glides into the vast darkness hovering beyond the moonlit lake. All my brothers settle into the night.

I make a wide loop, skimming the cushion of cool air above the black water. East, south, west and north. Skyward and earthward. As raven, and as woman, I exist in the six directions.

But there is a seventh. Yes, a seventh direction, and I have only just realized it. The rapid beating of my raven heart chants a truth that was never mine before. Within. Within. Within. There is a seventh direction, and it is within.

Gray Wolf arrives on the first offering day since my return from the mountain. Red paint covers his face and bands of red circle his elbows, wrists, knees, and ankles. But none from the village follow the sachem. There is no need for burden-baskets heavy with supplies—six human brothers are more than enough to provide for a family of eight.

My brothers have hunted and fished and made themselves known in the village. Their days as ravens were not wasted and they know the names and ways of many—including, it seems, the women. According to Little Trickster, Always First spends much time speaking with Two Feathers, while his avian eyes dart many times to Two Feathers' sister, Bright Star.

At night we are ravens and fly to the Hidden Lake. There, I search the woods and sky for my father, but never find him. I wish to tell him I regret my angry words. I wish to plead for the continued prosperity of the village. But all I can do each day as raven, and as woman, is live my life.

Always First addresses Gray Wolf. "Father of our village, we welcome you."

Gray Wolf returns the greeting with a nod of his head. "Grandmother Moon has shown her full face," he says, "and our crop continues to grow tall and strong. It is time to give thanks." He walks to the edge of the hill and raises his arms to Spirit Mountain.

I join Raven Keeper and my brothers in an arc behind him.

We look to Spirit Mountain as Gray Wolf chants the praise we all feel in our hearts.

"Great Spirit, we thank you for the people who move about on the earth. The people of our village do not know hunger or great illness, and we are grateful. The earth, our Mother, who supports our feet, cradles the roots of the trees and plants. We thank you for the trees and plants, for the food and medicine that they provide ..."

I stand between Proud Beak and Restless Lookout and look from one profile to the next. To the left, Proud Beak's smooth head curves into a nose that is as straight as his father's. To the right is Restless Lookout's fan of cropped hair. His bare ears twitch and beneath long lashes, his dark eyes dart and flicker. A sudden lift of Restless Lookout's brow startles me. I watch his eyes focus and follow his stare to the base of Spirit Mountain.

I think at first it is the shadow of a hill on the mountainside, but Grandfather Sun is too high for this to be so. The dark form grows and moves. I glance around me, but all eyes are still on the white peak of Spirit Mountain.

The mountain shadow rises like an otter from the water. A shrill hum mixes with Gray Wolf's voice. One by one, I feel the attention shift, until our collective awareness is focused on the black cloud rising above the hills.

Gray Wolf is the last to take notice. "...We give thanks to the Three Sisters—corn and beans and—"

The screeching trill increases as the black cloud approaches. No, not a cloud, but a solid mass. Closer it comes. Not solid, but many movements that make up one flowing, screaming form—a swarm of birds—thousands. Crows and grackles and redwings. Jays and chickadees and magpies. A fluttering hoard of hungry, eager, scavenging birds.

"No," I murmur. "No, no, no."

Proud Beak rests a hand on my shoulder and I am silent.

They fly above us and block the sun. It is as dark as dusk.

The pitch and volume of their calls is deafening. The constant motion of the fluttering, shrieking, living mass that circles above us is almost overwhelming.

This is the end of us. This is the end I have made. Here are the birds that will pillage our budding summer crop. Here are the birds sent by Man Who Is Raven. If I did not feel the strength of Proud Beak's hand on my shoulder, I would collapse into a motionless heap of grief and sorrow. But I remain, as we all do, with eyes lifted to the cloud of our destruction.

"Hear me," shouts a voice.

I gasp and spin around. Man Who Is Raven stands behind us. His hair flies in the shadow of the swarm. We have all turned to him—all but Raven Keeper, who keeps her eyes to the hills.

Man Who Is Raven's right hand grips a spear that is as high as his head. The wind whips six black feathers fastened in even increments along its shaft. Man Who Is Raven lifts the spear and swings it under his arm. He extends the blackened point toward me and calls above the racket. "Do you call me father?"

I swallow first, then fill my lungs and shout my answer: "I do."

Man Who Is Raven presses the spear above his head, lifts his face to the cloud of birds and roars through the wall of their noise. "Find the wild berries to sustain you. Find the worms and the crickets. This is my family. Where they plant, let them be. Do not eat their corn, their squash, their beans. Go now. Tell your cousins. Tell your children. I have spoken."

Winged creatures large and small—black, white, yellow, blue, and red—scatter in all directions. The light of Grandfather Sun shines again on our skin and the chirps and twitters return to a level of comfort and peace.

Relief, like warm molasses, flows through my body.

The long hair of Man Who Is Raven spills down his bare chest. The six feathers on the spear at his side flutter softly.

My father links his black eyes with mine. "You were the first to challenge me," he says. "The way you spoke—I saw myself in you—but something else too. Love. Compassion. Hunh! These did not make you weak. And so my heart is softened."

Raven Keeper turns then, for the first time, to look upon the man she once called husband.

Man Who Is Raven's wide-set eyes dart to her. He lifts the spear and thrusts its point into the earth near Raven Keeper's feet. "With love and respect have our sons obeyed me. Now I give their keeping to you. No longer are they bound to me." Man Who Is Raven releases the spear and with a slight tremor, it stands alone, between them.

Raven Keeper curls her fingers around the shaft. She grips it so that her knuckles whiten. A tiny shift in Raven Keeper's stance makes her seem taller, and she looks hard at the face of Man Who Is Raven. Not sadness. Not anger. My mother's face glows with peaceful triumph.

Then, for the second time, I watch my father become Raven. Unafraid, I enjoy the beauty of the transformation. Flesh to feathers. Face to beak. Legs to claws. My father takes to the air, curls his talons beneath his wedge-shaped tail, and in waves of fluid black flies to Spirit Mountain.

We watch him. Nine of us. Gray Wolf's eyes are wide. Raven Keeper's expression has not changed.

When Man Who Is Raven is gone from view, Raven Keeper uncurls her fingers from the shaft of the spear and, without a word, walks to the lodge. She reappears a moment later with a flint knife in her hand. She reaches up, cuts the topmost feather from the shaft and hands it to Always First. The second feather goes to Proud Beak and the third, fourth, fifth, and sixth to each of the rest of her sons.

Raven Keeper pulls the naked spear from the ground, holds it before her with two hands and with a swift motion breaks it across her knee.

I jump at the crack of the wood.

Gray Wolf's eyebrows are high. Even the sachem does not know what to expect. The six other men, each clutching a single feather, do not move.

Raven Keeper claps the dust from her hands. She looks twice at the group assembled near her, as if startled by her audience. When her eyes meet mine, she seems to sense the questions I hold tight in my chest.

"Each child of mine," says Raven Keeper, "was born with tiny fingers clutching a single black feather. When the child reached his first winter, Man Who Is Raven took that feather from me. The birth feather bound the child to him, and the father took the son then, as raven, whenever he wished. Watching my children leave each night gave me great sorrow, so when my sixth child reached his first winter"—her eyes drift to Little Trickster—"I hid his birth feather." Raven Keeper looks to the ground. "It was a mistake to invite the anger of my feral husband. He threatened to keep the rest of my children from me and so I relinquished the sixth feather, as he wished." My mother's eyes lift to mine. "After that, Man Who Is Raven did not trust me. When you were ... were taken from me, your father was blind to my grief. He was certain I had hidden you away—that someone from the village had helped me." Raven Keeper sighs and looks away, toward Spirit Mountain. "You have learned the rest."

I whisper my question. "And the feather? My feather?"

Raven Keeper's eyes sparkle. "Where it has been since you kicked your feet and cried for my breast."

The answer appears to me as suddenly as a rabbit from its hole. I run across the grass and plunge into the lodge. Inside, my feet are quick, but my eyes are slow to adjust to the dim light. I stub my toe on a fire stone, hop to the rear of the lodge, and almost fall into the human-size nest of sticks and earth. My fingers shake as they reach inside. I pull away the soft hide that lines the center and see it there. The black feather of my birth.

Holding my feather aloft, I make my way more carefully back toward the doorway. I blink at the sunlight as I emerge from the darkness and smile at the faces that gape with curiosity. Gray Wolf now stands a few paces apart from my brothers.

"It was there all along," I say as I run toward my family.

Raven Keeper smiles at my prize. "You were the only one never bound to him."

I run my fingers along the soft sides of the black feather. "Although," I say, "I had a very different bond to break."

"This is so," says Raven Keeper. She sweeps a hand across the assembly of her sons. "Now, like Sister Raven, you are bound to no one. Each must find his own path. Take your raven form when you wish." She holds them with her gaze a moment longer. "I advise you, though, that when you take a wife, to keep two feet always planted firmly on the ground."

Flies Too Far raises a fist in the air and emits a short celebration whoop. Proud Beak presses back his broad shoulders and Observes From Trees tilts his head in contemplation. Little Trickster's belly makes the sound of a hungry mountain lion, and we all laugh.

Raven Keeper addresses Gray Wolf. "Father of our village and friend to our family, please stay and share a meal with us."

Gray Wolf accepts the invitation with an easy smile.

I follow Raven Keeper inside the lodge, but before I help her to strengthen the fire and prepare the meal, I slip back to the bed that was mine for the first seven moons of my life. When I lift the berry-stained lining, the nest exudes an earthen breath that comforts me. I slip my feather back among the twigs and cover it again. If Old Mother had known my birth feather was hidden here, she could have ruled me longer. But not forever. Only the bonds of love, I think, can last forever.

After a hearty meal, Always First and Proud Beak follow

Gray Wolf down the hill toward the village. The thin braid that falls from the circle of hair on the back of Proud Beak's head dissects a tattoo on his back. The angled black lines form an image of a bird, with wings spread.

Observes From Trees rests by the fire inside the lodge. The raccoon tail falls across his shoulder as he leans forward to study his birth feather. Restless Lookout and Flies Too Far shed their human forms and take to the sky as ravens. Little Trickster walks into the woods as if he will fly away too, but jumps from behind the lodge to scare me as I select logs from the stack. As payment, I make him carry the firewood into the lodge for me.

"Perhaps tomorrow I will fly to the Hidden Lake," he says above the pile of dry branches in his arms. His birth feather, secured to his loose hair, dangles beside his face. "Will you fly with me, Sister?"

"No," I say. "I will not fly again."

Little Trickster's eyes open wide. "Never?"

"I have been Raven for a scattering of nights." I scoop up a handful of brown pine needles from the ground and inhale their scent. "Enough nights to know that my home is here, on the earth."

"Won't you miss it—the feeling of flight?"

"Ah, Brother," I say. "I do not need feathers for my spirit to fly."

The joyful pounding of drums shakes loose the spirit of the village. Flames as tall as cornstalks send sparks into the darkness and the smell of roasted meat and boiled squash linger in the air. Tap, step. Tap, step. Tap, step. Clouds of loose dirt float at the feet of the dancers who circle the fire. As stately as the grandmothers, or as wild as the young men, the village celebrates with one heart—one heart that beats to the sound of the drums.

Hey-ya! Hey-ya! Hey-hey-ya ho! Syllables, meaningless on their own, combine in voices that chant joy at the marriage feast.

A little girl, flushed with excitement, races past me. She knocks my elbow and a few drops of the corn gruel I hold splashes from the wooden bowl. I smile and watch her join in the dancing. She tries to imitate the twirls and gyrations of Little Trickster, but falls to the ground, laughing. No one can dance with as much skill and energy as my mischievous brother—a brother decorated, from head to toe, in swirling patterns of red and white.

Always First takes one last, exhausted hop, falls out of the circle of dancers and settles on the mat by his bride. Love and happiness shine in the eyes of Gray Wolf's daughter, Bright Star. It is a good match, and not the first that unites the family of Gray Wolf with my own.

Two Feathers, my husband, takes my elbow and spins me

around. His skin glistens with the effort of his own vigorous dancing and he shakes loose hair from his face. "How can you stand so still, my wife? Do you not hear the drums beg you to lift your feet?"

I balance the bowl, but corn gruel sloshes on my hands and drips to the ground. I laugh and tease him. "I have a husband who can only dance and waste good food."

He sniffs the bowl and wrinkles his nose. "I have a wife who does not know good food from bad."

Like a spark from the fire, Two Feathers flits away. He waves to Observes From Trees, to draw him out from the shadow of a lodge. Observes From Trees, with his raccoon tail dangling from disheveled hair, and a black band painted across his eyes, shakes his fist back and forth to say no. But Two Feathers does not accept that answer and drags his reluctant brother-in-law into the pulsating circle of dancers.

Little Foot smiles at me from across the fire. Little Foot's face is fuller since the birth of her child—not quite as pinched as it was before. Her husband is a man with a long neck and sloping shoulders, called Heron. At the Summer Festival, when her daughter was given a name, Little Foot presented me with the lighthearted gift of a smoked fish, and we have been good friends ever since.

There have been other celebrations since Man Who Is Raven lifted his shadow from the village—almost too many to count. We danced for the strawberries and then the green corn. We danced at my own marriage feast and then again at the Festival of the Harvest. Oh, how we danced for the harvest! A yield of abundance, thanks to the hard work of the women and the softened heart of my father.

But I have another parent—a mother I cannot disown. She lives in a small hut at the edge of the village. To the sound of drums and chanting, I bring her a bowl of corn gruel.

My hand lingers on the deerskin that covers the opening to

Old Mother's hut, as if I might open the doorway into the pain of my childhood. But the smoky fire and dirty mats do not belong to my life. And the old woman who sits in the shadows—I pity her.

"Listen, Old Mother," I say. "Do you hear the drums?"

"*Aye-kye*," says Old Mother. "So much noise."

"Shall I ask Gray Wolf if you might attend my brother's marriage feast?"

"Gray Wolf ... Gray Wolf," mumbles Old Mother. "How I suffer because of him! I am prisoner and outcast, both at the same time. He did this to me."

I do not remind her that she is not a prisoner, although without the magic of the bones she stole from Man Who Is Bear, Old Mother would never survive a journey alone. I also do not remind this unhappy woman that it was not Gray Wolf, but her own deceit and treachery that brought her to a place of dishonor in the village.

"Here is your supper," I say, and hand her the bowl. It is the bowl of burled wood, given to her as payment for healing a sick boy so many moons ago.

She reaches for her meal with bony fingers. Her fingernails are long and sharp and hair has grown thick on her gnarled hands.

Old Mother withdraws into the shadows. "Tasteless rubbish," she says between slurps. "This is all I get. Every day, the same." She pauses to add syrup to her tone. "Ah, my sweet daughter, perhaps you can bring me some dried berries. You don't mind that I call you daughter, do you? I was, after all, the one who cared for you all those years. I wanted you to love me. I tried—"

"I'm sorry, Old Mother. Corn gruel is all you are allowed. I add sugar when I can, do I not?"

"My life is a misery," grumbles Old Mother.

"You would not feel that way if you left this hut more often.

Grow your herbs again. Offer to help repair the fishing nets."

Old Mother leans her withered face into the firelight. Spittle forms at the corners of her mouth when she speaks and coarse hair surrounds her face. "I know how they talk of me. I would rather die than help those ungrateful women."

My only hope for Old Mother is that her heart finds a greater contentment when she walks in the Land of the Dead. Perhaps I should not have begged Gray Wolf for her life, but it did not seem fair to punish weakness with death. And so every day she eats corn gruel and curses the community that sustains her.

I push aside the door flap, stoop through the opening, and stand tall beneath the brilliant dome of starlight. I inhale the crisp autumn air through my nose and raise my face to Grandmother Moon. It is the time when she turns away a bit more every night, toward her dark night of rest.

I speak to the Grandmother above me, and also to the twisted woman behind. "I wish you peace."

Perhaps Old Mother heard. Perhaps she did not. I do not have time to wonder. In a blaze of red and white, Little Trickster charges out of the night, grabs my hand, and drags me, running, back to the boisterous center of the village. "You spend too much time with that one," he calls behind him.

Little Trickster hands me off to Raven Keeper, who waits with arms extended. Laughing, I stumble into her embrace, and together we join the women who stomp around the flames.

The circle pulsates and breathes as one. Tap, step. Tap, step. Tap, step. My feet beat the rhythm into the earth. *Hey-ya! Hey-ya! Hey-hey-ya ho!* The drums beat the rhythm into my heart. I dance to the drums and sorrow is a memory. I dance to the drums and I am complete.

Mother Earth sleeps beneath a white blanket, her loving womb heavy with our winter stores. It is the season when the river runs slow between ice-rimmed shores and the game is sparse, but easier to track. For most, it is a time of rest and rejuvenation, a time of meandering nights, story circles, and impromptu games of chance and skill.

But not for Two Feathers. And not for me.

We arrived at the village of the Twin Lakes two days ago, after a hard winter journey that lasted more than the cycle of a moon. There we found Old Mother's former husband, called He Who Walks Alone. This kind old man was happy to see me, for he had loved and cared for me when I was a toddler in his lodge. He Who Walks Alone made us welcome and after a restful night, directed us with words and signs to the object of our journey.

With each step, my snowshoes pack white powder. I bow my head against the cold, adjust my mittens, and pull the beaver hat closer about my ears. A shudder crosses my shoulders as I think of what might lie ahead.

Two Feathers trudges before me. He wears the hooded coat of rabbit skins I had crafted in the last winter of my loneliness—the same coat, wrapped in a bundle, that I had carried to the top of Spirit Mountain, and down again. I had given the coat and its contents to the Storyteller. That old man was Man Who Is Raven, who then snatched the bundle in his claws and flew away. After the harvest, I found the same coat outside Raven Keeper's lodge. I knew it to be an offering of peace and gratitude from my father, and stored it under a bench by the second fire, where I sleep with my husband.

"Look," says Two Feathers, and turns toward me. The hood frames his face. His cheeks glow red and ice sparkles on his lashes.

I follow the line of his arm and mitten to a broad oak, bare and disfigured. The forest opens to this tree and white stripes of snow rest across its branches.

Two Feathers tramps to the oak, breaks two long twigs from a drooping branch and holds one out to me. My snowshoes stamp the snow and I approach him, one sinking step at a time.

My husband reads my heart and looks long at me. His dark eyes say, *It must be done.*

I take the stick from him and together we poke the ground around the base of the oak. Each time we stab, our sticks measure a constant depth of snow. After a handful of scattered thrusts, my stick does not stop, but sinks until my mitten is swallowed in white.

"Here," I whisper.

Two Feathers lays his stone axe on the snow by his side, drops to his knees, and digs. Snow flies first, then wet, brown leaves, then hard, dark earth. He digs until the edges fall in and we look into the mouth of an underground void. Two Feathers inhales, then thrusts his stick into the black opening. Again, he jabs. And again.

My husband releases a long breath that lingers as an icy cloud and sits on his heels. The den is empty.

I recall Gray Wolf's words, spoken before we began this quest. "When you return his bones to the den, the spirit of the Strong One will be complete and he could find life again," my father-in-law had said. "Wait until the snow makes a white carpet and the hearts of the burrowing animals beat slow. Then such a being, who may be your enemy, might sleep."

I slide the mittens from my hands. Inside the rabbit-skin pouch that hangs from my belt, my fingers gather the bone knife and the beaded anklet. I expose these to the frigid air.

Uncertainty tightens my throat.

"What has been taken from you," I say to the open earth, "I now return. Thank you, Man Who Is Bear, for the healing that came from your bones and for the life-sustaining fires it ignited as I traveled with my husband." I drop the bone knife into the darkness. "Here are the bones that bound me for many winters to Old Mother. Thank you for their magic when it saved me from the mountain lion." The beaded anklet lies across my palm. My bare fingers tingle from the cold. "I am grateful also, Man Who Is Bear, for the lesson I learned as I cut this from my leg and broke a harmful bond." I toss the leather strip of tiny bones into the void.

In the time it takes for one breath, the earth trembles. The branches of the oak shiver and shed white powder. Two Feathers scoops up his axe and we stagger back, clumsy in our snowshoes. My racing heart tells my feet that they should race away too. But fear and fascination keep them still.

A grunt echoes inside the hollowed earth and a white vapor of warm breath drifts from the hole. Two Feathers shifts the axe in his bare hand.

A brown snout emerges and sniffs the air. A black head fills the width of the opening. The bear's eyes blink and shine and it retreats again into the den. I think that the bear will sleep and a sigh of relief passes my lips.

But my relief is short-lived.

With the sound of thunder, clumps of earth shoot into the air. I cover my head as stones and roots, balls of dirt and chunks of snow strike my arms and shoulders.

When the rain of earth is done, he stands before us.

Man Who Is Bear.

A long bearskin cape falls across his shoulders and a necklace of bear claws circles his thick neck. With shoulders as broad as the oak, Man Who Is Bear's presence fills the forest.

He stretches his arms and opens his mouth into a high-pitched yawn. Man Who Is Bear shakes his head so vigorously that his lips flap and his cheeks dance. He rubs his eyes and squints at me. "You there, are you—" He stops himself with a grumble, reaches behind his neck, dislodges the source of his discomfort, and throws it at the ground by my feet. It is the empty, broken handle of the bone knife. "No, no, you are too skinny," growls Man Who Is Bear, with his attention once again to me. "The woman I wait for is stout and looks always to the ground with humility and respect." Man Who Is Bear plants massive hands on his hips and laughs until his bare belly shakes. "Where is she, then? Where is the woman who promised to be my wife?"

Two Feathers and I exchange puzzled glances. "I ... I do not know this woman," I say.

"Not know her?" shouts the imposing man. "Not know the one who kept my bones?"

"Old Mother?" I ask. "Old Mother is to be your wife?"

Man Who Is Bear scratches his throat. "I see that for you, I must speak with the slowness of a turtle. Never mind. I will find her myself. Over three mountains would I know the scent of that she-bear." Man Who Is Bear gathers his robe around him and lumbers away. I hear the last of his words as he disappears into the forest. "I have waited many winters, but ah, she is worth it."

My husband and I stand for several moments, staring after the lustful giant.

Two Feathers breaks the silence with an explosion of laughter. He slaps his knees, falls sideways in the snow, and guffaws with his snowshoes in the air.

The image of Old Mother with that great bear of a man forms also in my mind. A smile travels to my lips and after one hiccupped chuckle, I too, lose myself in laughter.

I wipe the tears from my cheeks and Two Feathers takes my hand. Renewed by the power of relief and happiness, we slide our snowshoes across the winter powder and return to the village of the Twin Lakes by moonlight.

Tonight, above the lodge of my foster father, the tips of the pine trees create a jagged silhouette across the full face of Grandmother Moon. She seems close enough to touch and I bask in her maternal glow. "Soon," I tell her, "you will light my way home."

But Two Feathers and I will not make the journey to Raven Keeper's hill until the maples bud, the woodland is fat with birds and game, and the burden of travel is lighter. I reach my hand under my beaver-skin cape, press the hard roundness in the pit of my belly, and smile at Grandmother Moon. I am content to wait until the spring. But no longer. I will build my birthing hut close to my own village—in the place of my childhood, where I learned to fly.

Author's Note

It's difficult to categorize *Sister Raven*. I prefer to think of it as historical fantasy. The historical part of the novel is the culture and lifestyle of the pre-Columbian Native Americans who inhabited what is now New England. The fantasy, however, is completely of my own making.

I chose a fifteenth-century Native American setting because I felt it was the best fit for the mood I wanted to create and for the story I wanted to tell. I approached the historical research of the novel with diligence and respect.

It's important to note, however, that *Sister Raven* is not the retelling of a traditional Native American legend. The attitude toward the spirits of the earth, wind, and animals, and the reverence given to a Great Creator were common to the era, and many stories included animal shape-shifters, but to my knowledge, Sister Raven, Raven Keeper, and Man Who Is Raven were never part of the folklore.

In addition, many different tribes inhabited the area at that time. In order to avoid confusing my fantasy with individual tribal legends, I chose not to identify *Sister Raven* with any particular tribe.

This is a story of my own imagination, and it's my greatest wish for its readers, young or old, to find their own connection to it.

Karen Rae Levine